BETRAYING TRUST

SAM MASON K-9 DOG MYSTERY SERIES BOOK 4

L A DOBBS

This is a work of fiction.

None of it is real. All names, places, and events are products of the author's imagination. Any resemblance to real names, places, or events are purely coincidental, and should not be construed as being real.

~

Chief Sam Mason needs hard evidence to nail elusive drug dealer Lucas Thorne. Mayor Harley Dupont offers to provide it. But Dupont is murdered before he can talk.

Sam and Sergeant Jody Harris don't know who they can trust aside from their loyal K-9, Lucy. When the FBI comes sniffing around, their past actions come back to haunt them.

Just as Sam's strongest clue appears to be a dead end, a surprise twist reveals the truth behind Dupont's murder as well as the mysterious death of officer Tyler Richardson, and Sam learns that what he thought was a betrayal of trust was really something else entirely.

INTRODUCTION

Thanks for your interest in the Sam Mason Mystery Series! This series is set in small-town northern New Hampshire where anything can happen and playing by the rules doesn't necessarily mean that justice will be served. It features a small town police force and their trusty K-9 Lucy.

This is an on-going series with a completely solved mystery in each book and a lot of ongoing mysteries in the background. Don't forget to signup for my email list for advance notice on new release discounts:

https://ladobbsreaders.gr8.com

CHAPTER ONE

S am Mason stared at the photos of the bloody crime scene lining the corkboard in his office and reminded himself that sometimes, serving justice didn't always mean doing things by the book. Especially when you were the chief of police of a small northern New Hampshire town loaded with corruption.

He scrubbed his hand over his face, the rasping sound of the rough stubble on his chin reminding him that he was operating on only a few hours of sleep. He still wasn't caught up from the weekend stakeout that had turned out to be a waste of time.

"We can stare at these all we want, but they're not going to tell us who killed him." Sergeant Jody Harris stood beside him. Coppery curls sprang from under her navy-blue police cap, her gray eyes studying the photos intently. She had a yellow legal-sized notepad in one hand and a number-two pencil in the other.

"I know, but I keep hoping I'll see something that will give us a lead."

"We already know Thorne's behind this. And we have to prove it and take him down before he takes us down."

Jo was right. The crime scene had a lot of potential for things to go sideways for Sam and Jo. The victim, Mayor Harley Dupont, had requested a secret meeting with them the night he was killed. He'd promised to turn over information that would help incriminate Lucas Thorne. Sam desperately needed such information. He'd been trying to get something on the real estate developer, whom they suspected was responsible for the influx of drugs into White Rock for years now.

Trouble was, every time Sam thought he had a good sting in place, someone tipped off Thorne. Which brought him to the second piece of information Dupont had promised: something on fellow officer Tyler Richardson.

Earlier that summer, Tyler had been gunned down at what appeared to be a routine stop. It appeared as if he'd pulled over to help someone with a flat tire. But the case had turned strange. The facts didn't add up. The killer and the driver of the car were never found. The only solid clue was a lone fingerprint that didn't match any in the Automated Fingerprint Identification System database.

Dupont had claimed he had information about Tyler's death, which, as it turned out, could be another big problem for them.

Sam glanced back at the photos taken inside the abandoned mill where Dupont had requested the meeting. Dupont lay on the dusty, wide pine floorboards. Blood pooled under his head, and a gun lay at his side. Pigeon droppings splattered the scene as if someone had taken a brush and flung paint around.

Sam could still smell the dry wood of the old mill and hear the pigeons flapping in the odd hushed silence that always seemed to surround the dead. His eyes focused on one photo. Dupont's empty hand lay palm up, half curled. Dupont had been dead when they arrived, their only information on a small scrap of paper in the dead mayor's hand.

Had anyone noticed that paper was missing?

"I still can't believe that Tyler was tipping off Thorne," Jo said, as if reading Sam's thoughts about the missing piece of paper.

The paper, a scrap from a DNA test, indicated that their fellow officer and trusted friend Tyler was related to Lucas Thorne. The paper wasn't in the crime scene photos because Sam and Jo had taken it. And that wasn't the only thing they'd tampered with before the rest of the police arrived, which was why this investigation could become an even bigger problem.

Sam glanced back at the door to his office. Shadows moving beyond the smoked glass window set in the top portion of the antique golden-oak door indicated activity in the squad room.

Sam lowered his voice. "Maybe he wasn't."

"But those DNA results. There's no denying those," Jo whispered. "I would've bet my paycheck that Tyler was one of the good guys too."

Sam looked down at her and nodded. After Tyler had died, they'd done everything to protect his memory. They'd investigated the case in their spare time even though the state police had taken over and forbidden them from taking part in the investigation. Jo had even forged an entry in Tyler's logbook to make it appear as though he'd done everything by the book. But still, from the very beginning, something had been off. "It kind of makes sense now. We knew someone was feeding information to Thorne. That's why all our surprise busts didn't pan out."

"Especially the last one at the river. But Tyler was already dead. Who was feeding him information then?"

Sam shrugged. "I suspect Thorne simply felt things were too hot around here with the mayor's death just days before and called off the drop." They'd been tipped that Thorne was moving drugs out of state using a small river in a remote location. But a two-day stakeout at the most likely spot had yielded nothing. Sam figured Thorne had realized it was too risky to make a move so close to Dupont's murder.

"Probably. So how do we catch him? We've been over the crime scene countless times. We've scoured Dupont's house and his office."

Sam walked to the tall windows in his office and looked out at the quaint New England town, past the green of the commons and toward the brick building where Harley Dupont used to preside as mayor. Lucy, the German shepherd mix police dog, lay in a pool of early-morning sunshine on the honey-gold oak floor. She glanced up with one whiskey-brown eye then, upon deciding there was nothing of interest going on, snapped it shut and went back to sleep. "I just hope we're doing the right thing."

"We haven't done anything yet." Jo tapped the end of her pencil on her notepad. "Well, hardly anything. I mean, we did what we did for the right reasons."

The tense tone of her voice indicated she felt the same apprehension that Sam did about tampering with crime scenes. He reminded himself they were doing this for the right reasons. *They* were the good guys. But the way things had gone down with Dupont made Sam think Thorne might have seen an opportunity to silence the mayor and frame Sam for it.

Sam walked back to the corkboard, keeping his voice low. Only he and Jo knew what the crime scene had really looked like in that mill, and he wanted to keep it that way. "We have our work cut out for us, but finding the killer could lead us to Thorne."

"Whoever did this must be a close associate of Thorne's. If we can nail him for the murder, maybe we can convince him to give us evidence on Thorne's other activities." Jo glanced up at him. "I just hope a full investigation won't uncover some things better left covered."

"That's why I did a little rearranging." Sam cocked his head and looked at the photo of the gun next to the mayor, almost exactly as it would be positioned if he'd shot himself. *Almost.* "Gives us the opportunity to rule it a suicide." Sam didn't like the idea of not conducting the full investigation. He was all about justice. But in this case, what could come out in the investigation might not serve justice. Maybe Thorne had rigged things this way on purpose.

Still, he was having regrets about moving the gun. Tampering with crime scenes wasn't the norm for him. He had integrity. Principles. But sometimes you had to do what you had to do in order to get to the truth.

"Seems risky. What about the medical examiner and Kevin? We won't be the only ones looking at this case."

"John hasn't written up his report yet. He hasn't said one way or the other whether he thinks it's suicide or homicide. And Kevin, well, I think he seems on board with ruling it a suicide."

"How do you know that?"

"He indicated that when we were on the stakeout." Sam had been surprised that their part-time officer, Kevin Deckard, had apparently been well aware that Thorne might be setting them up. Kevin had come a long way in the few months since Tyler's death. Sam hadn't been so sure of his loyalties earlier in the summer, but he'd stepped up big time and gone above and beyond on the stakeout. Sam hadn't taken him into his confidence about what he'd done at the crime scene, though. The only one he trusted with that was Jo.

A knock sounded on the door. Sam shot a warning look at Jo, not that it was necessary.

"Come in," Sam said.

The door opened, and Kevin Deckard and Wyatt Davis came in. Kevin clutched a white bag of doughnuts from the local coffee shop, Brewed Awakening, in his hand.

"Hey, Chief. I've shown Wyatt the ropes." Kevin raised the bag. "Including the important parts, like where Brewed Awakening is."

"Thanks for coming in early, Wyatt." Wyatt wasn't supposed to start for two weeks, but given everything taking place with the investigation, they'd called him in to start that morning.

"No problem," Wyatt said. He looked at ease in his uniform. Proud to wear it. Maybe a little too proud. If he had an overly developed sense of his own authority, Sam would have to deal with that later. It wasn't as if applicants for this police job way up in the middle of nowhere were knocking down his door. Wyatt's had been the most qualified of the few resumes that had crossed his desk.

Kevin gave the bag to Jo. She peered inside and

pulled out a jelly doughnut then passed the bag to Sam.

The crinkling of the bag woke Lucy. She trotted over next to Sam and gazed up at him with hopeful eyes.

"Not today, buddy. These aren't good for you." Sam bit into a cruller and passed the bag to Wyatt.

"Any new ideas?" Kevin's eyes drifted to the corkboard. "I brought Wyatt up to speed on what we have so far."

Wyatt stepped in front of the board. "I hear the mayor wasn't well liked around here," he said without turning to face them, still studying the gruesome photos.

"Not really," Sam said. "He made upholding the law difficult for us."

"There was a reason. He was in deep with Thorne." Jo wiped a blob of jelly off her shirt.

"He wasn't a nice guy, either." Kevin put the doughnut bag on Sam's desk and bent down to pet Lucy. "If he had his way, we wouldn't have Lucy here as our K-9."

Wyatt turned, his dark eyes narrowed on the dog. "Animal hater?"

"Yep," Jo said.

"Probably made a lot of enemies," Wyatt said.

"No doubt." Sam leaned a hip against his desk and looked back at the photos. "Dupont had set up a meeting with Jo and me that night. He was going to hand us evidence we could use against Lucas Thorne. But when we got there, he was already dead. Dupont must have been getting nervous about what he had gotten himself into. Either he couldn't see any way out and took his own life, or Thorne got wind he was going to talk and took it for him."

Wyatt's eyes flicked to the photos. "You think it could be suicide?"

"Possibly. The gun was at the scene and in the right position," Sam said.

Wyatt cocked his head to look at a photo from a different angle, doubt seeping into his expression.

"If he was murdered, leaving the gun doesn't make any sense," Jo said. "Unless the killer had a reason."

"Like what?" Wyatt asked.

"To frame Sam or Jo." Kevin's words surprised Sam. Apparently, Kevin was much more insightful than Sam had thought.

"That would serve two purposes," Jo said. "Avoid being prosecuted himself and put someone in place here at the police station that he can control."

Wyatt nodded and reached down to pet Lucy, his face relaxing into a smile as his hands touched her tan-

and-black fur. Her tail swished on the floor. Sam's estimation of Wyatt went up a notch. Anyone who liked dogs was okay in his book.

Wyatt looked back up at them. "So, how do we prove it was him?"

CHAPTER TWO

Jody Harris sat in the hard oak chair that Sam liked to use when questioning suspects. He'd sawn a quarter inch off of one leg so that it tipped back and forth. Came in handy for throwing suspects off balance during interrogations. Not so handy for taking notes in a police investigation, as Jo was trying to do right now.

Sam was in front of his desk, one hip leaned against the edge. Kevin and Wyatt took up the other two oak chairs. Lucy was back in her spot in the sun.

It had been almost a week since the murder. They'd done a fairly thorough job of looking for evidence at Dupont's and had also interviewed all of his contacts. They'd been busy on the stakeout at the river where they thought Thorne would be making a drug drop, and that had eaten into time they could have spent investigating Dupont's death.

Jody glanced at the new guy, Wyatt. He seemed competent. She supposed he was good-looking, tall with a trim-cut beard. Not as tall as Sam or as broad, but he had a certain boyish appeal. Not that Jo was looking; Wyatt was ten years her junior, and she wasn't in the market for a man anyway. She appreciated that Sam had given her a chance to look at his resume and talk to Wyatt before making the final decision on hiring him. It made her feel like her input was important.

It was early yet, but Jo doubted she'd develop the same bond with Wyatt that she had with Sam and Tyler. Maybe that wasn't such a bad thing considering that Tyler had ended up being a traitor. Wyatt seemed competent, and they desperately needed the help. Hopefully, they'd click over time. And now that Kevin seemed to be coming around, they might have a pretty tight team in place.

Her gaze drifted back to Sam as he went over the specifics of the case. His navy-blue T-shirt was a bit rumpled, but he radiated an exciting energy even though the salt-and-pepper stubble that covered his chin and the lines etched into his face betrayed the fact that he must be as tired as she felt. Sam was a good cop, a loyal cop, a trustworthy cop, and Jo was proud to work under him, even if he pushed them, no matter how exhausted they were, to solve this case.

She glanced nervously again at the photos. Had it been a mistake to move the gun? There was no telling what Thorne had planned, and while neither of them wanted to obscure justice, they'd try to work the case so that the outcome was the same even if they had to take a circular route. If they thought it best to try to get a ruling of suicide, they'd continue their efforts to go after Thorne. Either way, Thorne would pay.

Whichever way Sam wanted to play it, Jo would go along, because she trusted him. Especially because he'd trusted her with his secret that night at the mill. A pang of guilt picked at her stomach. Problem was, she hadn't trusted Sam with *her* secret yet, and until she did, things wouldn't be open between them.

"So you don't mind doing that, Jo?" Sam's question pulled her out of her thoughts.

Jo's head shot up. "What?" The pencil tapping on her notepad increased.

"Making a few calls to some of the people Dupont met with the day before he died. Maybe one of them can give us some insight as to his frame of mind."

"Oh, yeah. Sure. I have a list from his assistant. Of course, most of his meetings were with Jamison."

Henley Jamison had been Dupont's vice mayor. He was now acting mayor and was almost as antagonistic as Dupont but maybe not quite as cautious. He'd already started to put pressure on them, just as Dupont had. Whether or not he would try to impede investigations that involved Thorne remained to be seen. Jamison was ambitious, but was he ambitious enough to get into bed with Thorne as Dupont had? It hadn't worked out very well for his predecessor.

"Okay, I'm going to go get together with John and go over his report," Sam said, referring to John Dudley, the county medical examiner. "Kevin, I want you and Wyatt to go over the crime scene at Reed's Ferry Mill again. But this time, search farther away from the building. I know it's contaminated there because it's been a week. I know the drug addicts are going back in, but maybe there's something out there. The killer might have parked on the access road and walked in. There're some narrow trails. Take Lucy. If something is there, she'll sniff it out."

At the sound of her name, Lucy lifted her head and gave Sam a questioning look, the fur on her forehead wrinkling above curious eyes.

Kevin sat up a little straighter in his chair and nodded. As a part-timer and low man on the pole, Kevin was usually relegated to grunt work. After

Tyler's death, they'd been shorthanded, and he'd had to step it up. At first, Jo hadn't been so sure about trusting him with extra responsibilities. She thought she'd even caught him lying once when she'd seen him come out of the alley near a restaurant. But he'd proved himself these last few weeks, and she was happy he was getting better assignments, even if she was a bit jealous that Kevin was getting to do fun field work while she was stuck making phone calls on this one. Sam always had a reason for everything, and she suspected that Sam was giving this job to Kevin and Wyatt so it wouldn't seem as if she and Sam were collecting all the physical evidence.

A knock sounded on the door, and the receptionist, Reese Hordon, poked her head in.

"Sorry, Sam. I got a call from Nettie Deardorff about Bitsy again. Seems the goat chewed up the hem of her new housedress that was drying on the clothesline."

Reese's expression was apologetic. Her long dark hair was pulled into ponytails that cascaded down the sides of her face. Her blue eyes looked at them keenly. Jo liked the young woman, who was a cadet at the police academy and had a good instinct for police work. Not to mention that her contacts at the academy sometimes allowed them to expedite things as well as glean sensitive information off the record. What Jo liked most about her was that Reese didn't flinch when they had to push the envelope a bit in order to expedite justice.

Lucy swiveled her head and wagged her tail furiously at the sight of Reese.

"Goat?" Wyatt asked.

"Nettie Deardorff is one of our senior residents. She's had a feud going on with her neighbor, Rita Hoelscher, as long as I can remember," Sam said. "They've fought over many things over the years, but ever since Rita got Bitsy—that's her goat—Nettie has really stepped up her complaints. Thing is, Bitsy does get out and chew on things. Sometimes I wonder if Rita lets her out on purpose. A few months ago, Nettie got a chicken, and now they take turns calling in complaints on the other's pets. It always ends amicably. I think they just want attention."

Kevin rose from his chair. "I'll take care of it."

Sam held his hand out. "You sit back down. This will be good experience for Wyatt. Get him used to the local folks and all."

Kevin beamed.

"Sure. I can handle that," Wyatt said.

"I have the address right here." Reese held a pink Post-it note out toward Wyatt.

Sam's gaze drifted out the window. "Crap."

Henley Jamison was walking down the sidewalk. It was a hot summer day, but he wore his charcoal-gray Armani suit coat, his crimson tie making a statement against his white shirt. Every single hair was perfectly in place as he strutted down the street in his shiny Ferragamo shoes toward the police station.

Sam pulled open his drawer and grabbed his keys. "Okay, let's wrap this up quick and get out of here before Jamison comes in and makes a pain in the butt of himself."

The office filled with the sounds of chairs scraping as they all jumped up and ran for the door. Sam's voice stopped them as Jo was reaching for the old brass doorknob.

"Let's do our best work today. We need to wrap this one up quick. I have a feeling Jamison might be ready to call in reinforcements, and I don't think any of us wants another police department getting into our business."

CHAPTER THREE

As Kevin turned into the parking area of the Reed's Ferry Mill, Sam's words echoed in his head. He sure as hell didn't want another department looking into this case. That might lead to investigating each of *them*, and that was the last thing he wanted. Especially considering what he'd been up to.

In the passenger seat of the police-issue Crown Victoria, Lucy stared out the window intently, her gaze focused on the abandoned brick building. Kevin chose his parking spot carefully. The parking lot had been claimed by tall grass, scrawny shrubs, and thick weeds. He didn't want the Crown Vic to get scratched, because it was a privilege to be allowed to drive it.

The police department had only two vehicles; the other was the Tahoe that Sam usually drove. When

Tyler had been alive, he'd driven the Crown Vic, and Kevin had to drive his own car. But once Tyler was gone, Kevin graduated to the Crown Vic.

Now that Wyatt had been hired on full-time, would Sam let him drive the official car and bust Kevin back down to his personal vehicle? Kevin didn't think so. He had seniority, and Sam respected that sort of thing. But he still didn't want to risk his privileges by getting the car all dirty and scratched.

Kevin pulled to a stop and took his keys out of the ignition before reaching into his pocket for one of the special treats for which he drove two towns over to purchase for Lucy. They were her favorite. The smell of bacon permeated the car, drawing Lucy's gaze to the treat in his hand. He fed her the treat and then patted her, taking comfort in the softness of her fur on his fingertips.

"You remember this place, right, girl?"

Lucy tilted her head. She'd been over the crime scene several times with Sam and Jo.

"Of course, you do. Let's give it another look. I know you can find something." Kevin got out of the car and came around to the passenger side to let Lucy out. Pride swelled in his chest. Lucy usually stayed with Sam or Jo, but today Sam had trusted him with the dog. He was making progress, becoming part of Sam and Jo's inner circle.

Kevin had gotten attached to Lucy. He enjoyed her company, and she seemed to understand him. Dogs just took you at face value; they never complained. Didn't stab you in the back either. You could trust a dog. People, not so much. Before Lucy had come to the department, Kevin had felt isolated. As a part-timer, he worked odd hours, and it always seemed as if Sam, Jo, and Tyler were in a special group and he was the outsider. Once Lucy came on the scene, he felt he had a friend. And now things were really looking up. His relationship with Sam and Jo was strengthening. Sam had been giving him more responsibility and had shown in several ways that he trusted Kevin.

There was no way he would betray that trust. He couldn't undo what he'd already done, but at least he could try to make up for his mistakes.

His thoughts turned to the mysterious contact who had asked him to relay information about what was going on in the station. It had started almost a year ago. He found notes in his mailbox and his car. He met with people in shadowy alleys. He'd almost been caught at it once and was forced to lie to Jo, making up a story about meeting his cousin who worked at the restaurant next to the alley when she'd seen him coming out of the alley after meeting his contact.

Sure, he felt guilty about that now, but he'd done all that before he knew the truth. He'd thought he was doing the right thing. At first, Kevin hadn't understood who was behind the requests. He thought the FBI was investigating Sam and Jo. Kevin knew the agency didn't always go by the book, so he assumed they were up to something shady and he was helping the authorities catch them.

Once he started to work with Sam more closely, he began to realize that was not the case. Whoever was pressuring him for information about Sam and Jo was up to something else entirely. He was sure Sam and Jo weren't doing anything underhanded. Sure, they used some unconventional methods, but sometimes that was what you had to do in order to get justice. Especially in a town like White Rock, where corruption reached as high as the mayor himself. And after what happened at the stakeout, Kevin had a sneaking suspicion the orders from his contact were coming directly from Lucas Thorne. It was no coincidence that the drug drop at the river never happened after Kevin leaked information about the stakeout to his contact.

They waded through the knee-high grass. He'd have to check Lucy for ticks thoroughly later. He didn't bother going into the building; they'd been over it many times already, and by now, the crime scene had been contaminated by the lowlifes who hung out inside the mill. The only things to be seen in there were dirty mattresses, used needles, and crumpled junk food wrappers. He could do without the stink of vomit, urine, and sweat. He figured Lucy could too.

Not to mention the piles of pigeon droppings and those noisy birds cooing and their claws scraping the rafters as Kevin tried to work the scene. One of them had expressed its displeasure at his presence by splattering a fresh drop on his black police boots. That stuff was caustic; it had taken the shine right off that quarter-shaped spot. Nothing Kevin tried could restore the luster.

Kevin walked slowly, his eyes scanning the ground. Lucy ran ahead, sniffing every tree and acorn and scaring off a few squirrels, which chattered at her angrily from the branches they'd taken cover in.

It was hot, one of those sticky end-of-summer days. A bead of sweat trickled down the back of Kevin's neck as he swung his head back and forth, searching for anything that looked out of place.

He wondered if Sam would try to rule the investigation a suicide. He thought Sam might have a few reasons to do so. When Kevin had gotten to the crime scene, he'd noticed some discrepancies, like the smudge near the gun. He was pretty sure someone had moved it, and the only people who had been there were Sam and Jo ... and the killer. But why would the killer move the gun? Just in case, Kevin had obliterated the telltale smudge with the toe of his boot when no one was looking. He didn't want Sam to get into trouble.

The other discrepancy Kevin had noticed was the way Dupont's hand had been curled, as if he'd been clutching something. Kevin had to wonder if Sam knew more about that than he let on. But Kevin had his own reasons for wanting Dupont's death to be ruled a suicide. An investigation might uncover some of the things he'd been up to, like tipping Thorne off to police activity.

Passing information along wasn't the only thing he'd done. His contact had asked him to look through Tyler Richardson's belongings after his death. Kevin hadn't found anything except a thumb drive. Now he was glad he hadn't passed that drive along. Even though he hadn't found any files on it, special forensics might be able to recover previously erased data. He'd kept it as an insurance policy in case things went south.

But what was on it? Could it be something that

incriminated Thorne or something that incriminated Sam and Jo? Or it could be nothing. Better to keep it safely hidden away until his hand was forced.

He would never have to use it unless the investigation dug too deep. Yep, a suicide ruling was probably best. But Kevin had a funny feeling that not everyone might be willing to let it go as a suicide. The way Wyatt had been looking at those photos in Sam's office told Kevin he might not go along so easily. And he'd asked a lot of questions about Sam earlier that morning when Kevin had been showing him the ropes. He'd also indicated he didn't think that Dupont fit the suicide profile. Would he push back if Sam tried to press for a suicide conclusion?

Maybe that was just normal curiosity and Kevin was being paranoid. Still, there was something about Wyatt that tweaked Kevin's alarm bells. He couldn't quite put his finger on it. Maybe he was simply jealous that a new person was coming in just when he was finally making headway into Sam and Jo's confidence.

No, that was stupid. Sam had been giving him more responsibility. He'd let him handle the arrest of that environmentalist guy, and they'd bonded at the stakeout. Plus, Sam had picked him to take Lucy to the crime scene and sent Wyatt to deal with a local dispute. They were building trust, and a new guy wasn't going to jeopardize that.

Whether Dupont's death ended up a suicide or not, Kevin needed to find a clue that would lead them to Thorne. Once Thorne was out of the picture, Kevin wouldn't have to worry about his contact. And he was sure Thorne was the main source of the drug supply, judging by the generous amounts of money he was paid to tip him off about the police station happenings. Kevin was determined to make up for all the information he'd passed along, and the best way he could think to do that was to help nail Thorne.

Kevin whirled at the crunch of gravel to his left, his hand going automatically to the gun on his hip.

A thin old man with a smattering of gray hair crowning a shiny bald spot stood twenty feet away. A mixture of surprise and fear spread on his face as his eyes flicked from Kevin's face to the hand hovering above his gun. Kevin relaxed. It was just a civilian dressed in a yellow T-shirt and grass-stained tan chinos. He'd probably been mowing his lawn, judging by the clumps of grass on his sneakers.

"Boy, you cops sure take an active interest in this old mill," the man said.

"We're investigating," Kevin said. He was sure the man knew the mayor had been found dead inside the mill less than a week ago. It had been all over the news. "You live over there?" Kevin jutted his chin toward the neighborhood that he knew to be beyond the woods. If he lived there, how had the man seen him here?

The man shook his head and held out his hand. "Harvey Noonan. I live down the access road that way." The man pointed toward the dirt entrance road to the mill. "House is kind of secluded. Saw the police car drive by and wondered what was going on. Neighborhood's gone to shit with the drug addicts that come and go. And now a death."

Kevin walked closer and shook Harvey's hand. "You saw me drive by. You kind of watching the place?"

"Could say that. Can't be too careful." The man glanced warily at the mill.

"Did you see anything the other night or maybe that day?" Kevin asked. Sam, Jo, and Kevin had talked to all the neighbors, but Kevin hadn't talked to this one. He was probably one of the people Sam or Jo had talked to, but it didn't hurt to ask again. Sometimes people clammed up when they were being asked officially, or they simply didn't remember things until later.

"Lots of cops coming and going."

"You mean after we found the body?"

The man shook his head. "No. Not then, before."

"Before? How long before?"

"Earlier that afternoon."

Sam and Jo had had a meeting with Dupont that night, so they'd been here before all the sirens, but of course this neighbor didn't know that. "You mean right before you heard the sirens."

The man screwed up his face. "Are you daft? No wonder this town's gone to shit with you protecting it. I said earlier in the afternoon. I wouldn't bother to mention if it was *right* before. Of course the cops had to come here on some sort of call. This was *hours* before. I saw a car drive by and figured there were some goings on, but when I came down, it was just that lady cop. She was going in the building. I don't want to go anywhere near there, so I turned around and went back home."

Kevin frowned. Jo? Why had she been here earlier in the afternoon? He guessed it made sense. She'd probably come to scope the place out so that they'd have an exit strategy in case Dupont's meeting was an ambush. Yep, that made perfect sense. But if that was the case, why hadn't Sam or Jo mentioned that in the reports?

"Right. Well, the police are watching this place. Like you said, there's a lot of drug activity, and we want to keep the neighborhood safe, so we check in every so often," Kevin lied. He wanted to make an excuse for Jo, because if Sam and Jo hadn't mentioned her being here earlier, he was sure there was good reason for it.

The man screwed up his face and thought a minute. "Yeah. Right. That makes sense. That what you doing now?"

"That and looking for clues." Kevin pointed to Lucy.

The man nodded. "Okay, then. Hope you catch the guy that did it."

Kevin watched the man leave until he disappeared around the corner.

Kevin hoped Harvey wouldn't make an official report about what he'd just said. No one needed to know that Sam and Jo had omitted the part about her being there earlier in the day. It might have been an honest mistake, but official investigations could get sticky, and honest mistakes could get twisted out of context. Kevin would keep that information to himself.

Lucy's excited bark brought his attention back to the task at hand. She stood at the edge of the woods where a narrow trail started. She looked back at Kevin and then at an oak sapling in front of her. Her nose was high in the air, a position that Kevin had come to recognize as a sign that she'd sniffed out something of interest. Kevin knew that dogs had a strong sense of smell, but in the short time he'd worked with Lucy, he'd noticed that hers seemed almost as if it had been developed to an extraordinary level.

Kevin jogged over. "What did you find?"

Lucy pointed her ears forward and looked up at a leaf at about waist height. Kevin's eyes followed her gaze. The sapling had bright-green leaves, but the one Lucy looked at was stained with a rusty-brown smudge. He bent closer, his heartbeat picking up a notch. The smudge was the color of dried blood. A fingerprint? He couldn't see any whorls, but it was the right size.

Was that Dupont's blood? Was it from the killer? And if so, should he bag it as evidence, because if they were going to close this as a suicide, how could there be a fingerprint from the killer on a leaf? Maybe he should destroy it.

But if for some reason Sam decided to investigate, this fingerprint could come in handy, and he couldn't guarantee that he would come back to find it washed off by rain or devoured by bugs. He could put it in his evidence bag and hold it just in case, but then how would he explain coming back here to find it?

He took the evidence bag from his pocket and

turned it inside out. It was better to turn the print in. It might help them find the person doing Thorne's dirty work. If Sam decided to go the suicide route, they could always use it to prove that one of Thorne's minions had been here after the mayor killed himself. And that proof might be the thing that could help them build a case against Thorne, no matter what route they decided to take in the investigation of Dupont's death.

CHAPTER FOUR

S am didn't like the way things were going with John Dudley, the medical examiner. They stood side by side in the basement morgue. The temperature was set on chill, the room all stainless steel and gleaming white tile. The caustic smell of antiseptic and death permeated the air. Sam would never get used to that smell. Apparently, it didn't bother John. He seemed downright gleeful as he pointed to an x-ray of Dupont's head on the lighted display box.

"The bullet came in at this angle." John tapped on the x-ray then pointed to a photo of the crime scene that sat inside an open manila folder. "The angle just doesn't coincide with the way the gun fell. I had those fancy CSI yahoos up at the county crime lab reenact it. You know they have all kinds of gadgets to do that with. 'Course, there wasn't even a hint of a fingerprint on the gun."

"I know," Sam said. Sam should've known that John would consult with the county lab. He kicked himself for moving the gun in the first place. What had he been thinking?

"Right. Well, I have to admit I'm baffled as to why the gun was there. Dupont didn't do it, so it must have been the killer. But why?" John asked. "Another thing was the way Dupont's pocket was half out. Like he'd been handing something to the killer. Or the killer took it."

Sam gritted his teeth. This could be a complication. They'd searched Dupont at the mill hastily before anyone else had arrived. He hadn't mentioned that in his report.

"Maybe the killer was looking for cash, got scared off when he heard us coming in, and dropped the gun," Sam suggested.

John shrugged. "Maybe. Seems more like he planted it there."

Sam raised a brow. "Planted?"

"Yeah. Maybe he wanted the scene to look like a suicide, or maybe he wanted to set someone else up for it."

"Yeah, that thought did cross my mind." Great,

now he'd lied to John. Technically, it wasn't a lie. Sam did think he was being set up, and maybe that was the reason the killer had left the gun. He never should have moved the gun. But John had one thing right: it was odd the gun had been left behind. There was only one reason—to frame someone. Sam feared that *someone* was him.

Sam took the autopsy file from John and drove back to the police station. There was no question now. He'd be investigating Dupont's death as a murder.

Worried about what might be uncovered officially once he followed the case through properly, Sam trudged up the granite steps to the brick police building and pushed the double doors open. Reese scowled at him from behind an old metal teacher's desk they'd appropriated when the junior high had been renovated.

"I'm going to get back at you all for leaving me here with Jamison," the receptionist warned.

Sam shrugged, sheepish. "Sorry about that. But that guy can really impede things. I didn't want to get caught up in an argument with him. We have work to do."

"He was asking all kinds of questions. Digging into the specifics of what you guys were up to. Asking about private conversations. As if I'd tell." Reese rolled her eyes.

Sam smiled. "Thanks." He trusted Reese. She wouldn't let Jamison or anyone else know the details they wanted to keep secret.

"But I *am* going to get back at you." Reese's gaze drifted over Sam's shoulder. "In fact, that's going to happen any minute. Harry called, and I told him you'd love to see him."

"What? Please tell me you're joking." Sam spun around to see Harry Woolston walking up the steps. His sharp blue eyes sparkled under bushy white eyebrows that matched the thick shock of hair on his head.

Harry had been police chief when Sam was just a boy. He had to be pushing eighty. He liked to come in and relive his glory days. Usually, that consisted of meddling in Sam's investigations, though sometimes he did help out. But right now the last thing Sam wanted was Harry's help.

Too late for that. The door swung open, and Harry stepped in. "Sam! How's it going? You making headway in the Dupont case?"

"A bit," Sam said.

Harry smiled at Reese and handed over a box of chocolates. Sam's frown deepened. The last thing he needed was Reese falling under Harry's spell. Even at his age, he was a charmer. Sam didn't need Reese making it inviting for Harry to stop in every day.

"You ask me, the town is well rid of that Dupont character. Never liked that guy. Marnie Wilson's the one we need for mayor. And she's taken a shine to you." Harry winked at Sam and then took a chocolate from the box Reese had opened and bit into it. He frowned. "But we might've gone from the frying pan into the fire with that Henley Jamison in charge now. I only wish the election was sooner. The sooner we have it, the sooner we can get rid of the current riffraff."

"Can't argue with you there," Sam said.

The door opened again, and Wyatt stepped in. He looked surprised to see them all standing in the lobby.

"Hey. What's going on?"

"Nothing," Sam shifted to the left to accommodate the newcomer. The lobby was getting a little crowded. "We all just got here at the same time."

Harry stuck his hand out. "You must be the new guy. I'm Harry Woolston, chief of police."

Wyatt's questioning eyes flicked from Harry to Sam.

"Former chief," Sam said. "Did you take care of Nettie and Rita?"

"Yeah. They're very interesting."

"You must've made quite an impression on Rita," Reese said. "She called the station to put in a good word for the 'nice young man' who came out. Said something about bringing you fruitcake?"

Wyatt turned red. "Yeah. In order to get them to reconcile, I had to sit down with them for a slice of fruitcake."

Harry laughed. "You actually like that stuff?"

Wyatt grimaced. "No, but you gotta do what you gotta do to keep the peace."

They all laughed as the door opened again. Kevin and Lucy came in, and Sam shuffled another foot to the left.

Kevin stopped at the door. Lucy inched her way around the room, sniffing everyone's shoes.

"Hey, Harry, What's going on?" Kevin asked.

"We're just catching up on the case," Harry said. "Got any suspects?"

"We're not catching up on the case," Sam said. "At least *you're* not."

"I might have some ideas that could help you out." Harry leaned in closer. "You ask me, that Lucas Thorne is behind it."

"Why do you say that?"

"Come on, Sam. Everyone knows he's a bad seed. The way he's putting up all those buildings. Ripping down trees. Ruining our pristine town. And we all know Dupont was in his pocket. Why else would all those zoning laws be changed when no one in town wanted them changed? Dupont probably saw he was getting in too deep and wanted out, so Thorne removed him. Marnie Wilson will rein Thorne right in, though. He'll be as afraid of her as he is his wife."

Kevin's eyes narrowed. "He's afraid of his wife? Somehow I don't picture that."

Harry snorted. "I know, right? But that Beryl, she's a hard woman. Known her family for decades. That's how Thorne found our town; she brought him here. Beautiful woman but hard. Rich too." Harry's face turned thoughtful. "That's probably why he married her. For the money. Her family funded all his real estate development. Good match, though. She's the only woman devious enough to handle him. Smart— well, other than marrying Thorne. That's why she made him sign the prenup. She wears the pants in the family."

Sam exchanged a glance with Kevin. He couldn't picture Thorne yielding to a woman, but he'd never met Beryl. Sam tried to avoid Thorne whenever possible. He was a bit happy, though, to know there was someone who intimidated Thorne. Maybe Sam would take the wife out to lunch to show his approval.

The door opened again, and they all shuffled side-ways to accommodate Alvin Ray, the mailman. He was dressed in his usual meticulously pressed blue-and-gray uniform and carrying the white plastic box that he used to deliver bulk mail.

He stopped just inside the door, his brows raised. "Well, good morning. I'm not used to such a reception."

"Morning, Alvin," Harry said. "You're looking fine today."

Alvin smiled proudly. He was known for taking pride in his appearance. "Thank you!"

Alvin hefted the box onto Reese's desk, almost knocking the chocolates off. Harry pushed in between Wyatt and Alvin to catch them.

"*Hachoo!*" Harry sneezed.

Reese glanced up at Harry, her eyes wide with concern. "Harry, you coming down with something?"

"Nah," Harry scoffed, whipping out a white linen handkerchief and blowing his nose. "I never get sick. Allergies. Pet dander. Cats usually, maybe dogs too." He looked down at Lucy. "You been hanging around with any cats?"

Lucy narrowed her eyes and curled the left side of her lip as if the very idea of hanging around with cats was repugnant.

Harry grabbed another chocolate and sniffled. "Guess I better be moseying off. Wife wants me to pick up some lady stuff at the pharmacy."

Kevin turned sideways to let Harry get to the door, and they all watched him leave.

"Nice man," Alvin said as he sorted the mail onto Reese's desk.

"He is," Reese said.

"Coming in here always brings back fond memories." Alvin finished his sorting and looked around the lobby.

It had been only a few years since the post office moved to a new modern building and the police station was upgraded from the basement of the town hall to the old post building. The building still had all the original trappings, from the marble floors to the wainscoting to the oak doors with their etched-glass windows. They even made use of the mission-style furniture that had been in the building since 1930. It still smelled of years of lemon pledge and stamp glue. Some might have been put out by having to make do with the post office castoffs, but Sam thought the building and furnishings had character.

"Don't know why they put all that modern stuff in the new post office building. It just doesn't have the charm." Alvin waved toward the wall of post office boxes that divided the room. The antiques were constructed of solid brass, with black dials and eagles emblazoned below the small etched-glass windows. "Like these boxes. The new ones are just plain steel. So boring." Alvin squinted over the tops of the boxes into the squad room, his eyes darting to the corkboard where photos of the Dupont crime scene were tacked up.

He averted his gaze quickly. "Guess you guys are busy, what with what happened to the mayor and all." He pushed his black-framed glasses up on his nose.

"Sure are," Sam said.

Alvin turned toward the door, his face thoughtful. "Funny thing, though. What was the mayor doing in the mill? It's not really a place where someone like him should be."

"He might have been lured there or had a meeting. We're not sure yet." Sam had no intention of letting it get out that the mayor was meeting with them to provide information on Thorne.

Alvin shrugged. "Could have been a setup. You know, like on TV. There's rumors. But then I also heard rumors the only people seen there that day were the cops."

"We patrol that area from time to time," Sam said.

Alvin pushed his glasses up again. "Yeah, guess

that makes sense. Anyway, rumors are just that—rumors. Well, have a nice day."

The lobby was silent as they watched Alvin leave, his white sneakers squeaking on the polished marble floor as he swung open the door and exited into the sunlight.

As Sam watched him amble down the granite steps, Jo's voice rang out from the squad room.

"Are you guys going to sit out there, chatting like old ladies, all day, or you gonna come in here and help me solve the case?"

THE SQUAD ROOM wasn't big, but it was enough for the three desks that the department needed. Jo sat at hers next to the window, her laptop open, yellow smiley face coffee mug perched beside it.

As they filed into the room, she stood and came around to sit on the front of her desk, which faced into the middle of the room.

Kevin's desk was on the opposite wall. He pulled the chair out from under it and spun it around. Sam went to the coffee machine, popped an orange K-Cup of Gorilla Organic into the top, and started the machine. "Anybody want a coffee?"

"I'll take one," said Wyatt, standing beside him. "I like the strong stuff."

Sam nodded approvingly and made the two coffees, putting them in navy-blue White Rock Police Department mugs.

"That was kind of weird what the mailman said about a setup." Wyatt took his mug and looked at Sam. "You think this could be some kind of setup?"

"You never know. With Thorne, it's likely."

"You really think it's this developer guy?"

"Yep." Sam walked the few steps into the squad room. "You stick around long enough, you'll see why."

"So what'd you find out from John?" Jo's legs dangled in front of her desk, and she tapped her heels impatiently against the solid oak front. Their eyes met, and Sam could tell what she was thinking. She was wondering if John had evidence that indicated it wasn't a suicide. Might as well give her the bad news right away.

"John doesn't think it was a suicide. The placement of the gun isn't conducive to that." Sam hitched his hip on the corner of Kevin's desk and sipped his coffee.

Wyatt stood awkwardly in the center of the room. Sam hadn't yet assigned him a desk. The other desk was the one Tyler Richardson had occupied.

Sam nodded at Wyatt and gestured toward Tyler's desk. "You can take that desk." A pang of sadness speared him, but he'd have to get used to someone else sitting at Tyler's desk. Besides, as they'd recently learned, maybe Tyler wasn't as worthy of Sam's feelings as he'd once thought.

Wyatt looked at the desk uncertainly then sat behind it, facing them.

Lucy trotted over and sat in front of Jo's desk, looking up at the doughnut bag perched on the corner. Jo opened the bag and tilted it toward the dog. "Sorry, it's empty." She crumpled the bag and tossed it into the trash can next to the coffee maker.

"I'm not surprised. I didn't think it was suicide. Didn't look like it." Wyatt's voice was neutral, but the flicker of suspicion in his eyes put Sam on alert. Sam made a mental note to be cautious around Wyatt until he had him figured out.

"There were some discrepancies at the crime scene. But we have to do our due diligence and consider all the angles," Sam said.

Wyatt nodded.

Sam turned to Jo. "Did you get anything from his contacts?"

Jo shook her head. "I hightailed it out the back door when we saw Jamison coming. I figured it was a perfect opportunity to talk to Dupont's assistant without Jamison getting in the way. But she didn't have anything new to add, so I skedaddled out of there before Jamison returned. I came back here, and I've been calling the people on his calendar. We already talked to most of them, but I figure sometimes people think things over and remember something new. A few said he seemed a little nervous, but that makes sense given that he was having that secret meeting with us. Other than that, I didn't come up with anything new."

"I might have something." Kevin pulled an evidence bag from his pocket and held it up. Inside was a green leaf.

Sam squinted at the bag. "You found that at the mill?"

"Lucy found it, actually. Looks like there might be a blood smear on the leaf." Kevin handed it over to Sam, who held it up to the light.

"Could be unrelated to the murder. Lots of lowlifes hang out there, and who knows what kinds of things they get up to. Fights, maybe. But we'll see if the lab can get a print off it." Sam turned and called for Reese, who appeared around the side of the post office boxes. He handed her the evidence bag. "Can you get this to the lab and see if they can get a fingerprint or something off of it and test to see if it's blood? If it is, have them check to see if it's Dupont's."

Reese took the bag and held it close to her face, squinting. "I don't see any fingerprint, but it's the right shape. We learned about this last semester. I have a friend from school who is interning at the lab. I'll see if I can put a rush on it." She disappeared back out into the lobby, and Sam turned back to the others.

"Okay, you guys know the drill. We're treating this like any other homicide now. Everything by the book. We'll be under extraordinary scrutiny. Kevin and Wyatt, I want you to question the druggies who hang out at that mill building. There was no one there when we found Dupont, but maybe they were there before. Whoever killed Dupont might have been waiting for him, and someone may have heard or seen something."

Kevin stood and grabbed his keys. "We're on it."

"Jo, I want you to keep on that list. Go back to last week. Check out Dupont's neighbors. Maybe somebody saw someone coming to the house or something suspicious that day."

Jo slid off the desk. "Will do."

Sam started toward his office, catching Jo's eye on the way. Now that there was no question about the direction of the investigation, they would have to be careful, especially given what they'd learned about

Tyler. What they'd done to protect his name could come back to bite them.

Hopefully, they could keep anything about Tyler from coming out in the investigation. For some reason, Sam still didn't want his betrayal revealed. For one, he didn't want Tyler's memory spoiled for his elderly mother and disabled sister, Clarissa. Tyler had been a hero in their eyes, even moving in with his mother so he could use his check to pay for Clarissa's expensive treatments.

Jo fished her keys out of her desk and followed Sam to the office. "Now what? We need a plan."

Sam nodded. "I'm hoping we can play it by the book. We know who's behind this."

Jo lowered her voice to barely above a whisper. "And if certain things come to light in the investigation?"

"Maybe it's good if we go over things and think them through from all angles. Not here, though." Sam glanced at his door. He couldn't risk anyone over-hearing them. "Tonight. My house."

Jo nodded and turned toward the door.

"And Jo," Sam called to her as she got to the door.

She turned back to look at him. "Yeah?"

"You bring the beer."

CHAPTER FIVE

The day had yielded a big fat nothing. Sam had spent the afternoon trying to call in favors from his contacts in an attempt to home in on who Thorne would have ordered to kill Dupont. His contacts either didn't know, or weren't saying. Sam couldn't blame them. No one wanted to cross Thorne. He was a cold-hearted killer.

When he drove home that night, all he had was a smoking gun and a smudged leaf. But he had an idea about someone else he could press for information, an informant he'd been grooming for a while now. That person probably wouldn't know who was closest to Thorne in his chain of command, but he'd know the lowest link in that chain. Sam would have to start at the bottom.

Sam lived in an old log hunting cabin deep in the woods. His grandfather had built it, and the sight of the golden logs and wide front porch nestled between pines, birch, and oaks always brought him comfort.

He pulled into the driveway, and Lucy bounded out of the Tahoe and onto the porch. The green wooden rocking chair—his grandfather's favorite—rocked slightly as she sped past. She waited at the door, glancing back at Sam impatiently.

"You want dinner?"

Lucy wagged her tail furiously and gave him a look as if to say, "Duh."

Sam opened the door, and Lucy rushed to her stainless-steel bowl in the kitchen. Sam tossed his keys on the cedar log table beside the door and let the day's stress roll off. The cabin was still decorated exactly as it had been when his grandparents lived there: rustic, comfortable furniture, happy childhood memories, and the scent of cedar.

Sam poured the dry dog food the vet had recommended into Lucy's bowl then looked around the cabin. Grandma hadn't been much for decorating. She'd hunted and fished right alongside Sam's grandfather. In fact, one of the big taxidermy rainbow trout hanging on the wall was one she'd caught in the Sacagewassett here in town.

The warm log walls were dotted with other taxidermy and paintings of lakes and mountains in sunset pink, orange, and blue. The furniture was mostly hickory or birch. An oak china cabinet housed about the only items that couldn't be described as rustic: some of Grandma's old blue china. The cabin might not make *Architectural Digest,* but to Sam, it was perfect. It was home. Though it was a little messy right now. He supposed he should pick his socks up from under the coffee table and put away the T-shirt draped over the kitchen chair. Sam didn't socialize much with Jo outside of work and unwinding at Holy Spirits, the downtown bar built from a decommissioned church. Heck, he didn't socialize much at all, which was why the place was a mess. He never really had to pick up for anyone.

He'd just finished sprucing up and pouring some chips into a bowl when a soft tap at the open screen door brought his attention to the front of the house. Jo stood tentatively outside the door, holding a six-pack of Sam's favorite Moosenose beer.

The fading sunlight made her copper curls shine. Sam felt a rush of emotion. He was a solitary guy and didn't have many friends. Jo was one of the few people he trusted. One of the few people he could share things with. And now that they were in this mess together, it solidified that bond even more. He felt closer to Jo than he had to either of his two wives. That was probably because their relationship was purely platonic. Once you got romantic, things turned squirrelly. Luckily, that would never happen with Jo. For one, it wouldn't be appropriate because she was his second-in-command. Two, he couldn't risk losing her.

"Come on in," Sam said. Jo swung the door open and strode into the cabin, a smile flitting on her lips as she looked around.

"I always liked this place." Jo handed the six-pack to Sam, pulling one of the tall green bottles out for herself. "I think your grandma had style. It's comfortable."

Sam glanced around. Most women thought the cabin was a man cave. His ex-wife had refused to come here at all after Sam had inherited it. She preferred to stay in a fancy Victorian closer to town. As soon as the divorce was final, he'd sold that place and moved to the cabin. But it figured Jo would like it. She wasn't like most women. She was practical and earthy.

"Thanks. I like it." Sam gestured toward the couch, and Jo sat. Sam took the chair beside the couch and popped the top off his beer before handing the opener to Jo. Lucy trotted to Jo and sniffed and wagged her tail as Jo ruffled her behind the ears.

"So, I guess we'll need to conduct a full investigation after all," Jo probed.

Sam leaned forward, resting his arms on his thighs, the beer clasped in both hands. "Yeah. I guess we should have known that suicide thing wouldn't fly. Probably never should have moved the gun."

"I don't think that will be too much of a problem. Who's to know that the killer didn't put it there?" Jo took a sip of beer. "What I don't get is why the killer left the gun in the first place."

"I think Thorne is up to something. Maybe there is something on the gun and he's trying to frame someone."

"Yeah, like us."

"The gun is still at the crime lab. Ballistics reported it was the weapon that killed Dupont. So far, there's nothing else. But we don't know what else Thorne has in store."

"That's why we need to solve this fast. We need to be able to maintain control of the investigation."

Sam picked at the label on his beer. "Might be hard with Kevin and Wyatt. We have to be careful about which aspects we investigate and which they investigate."

Jo sighed and pushed up from the couch, running her hand through her mass of curly hair. "You know, it shouldn't be this hard. We didn't do anything wrong. We were only trying to protect Tyler's reputation."

"I know. And then to find out he's related to Thorne ..."

"Did you ever get the report on the DNA from the lab? Could we be wrong about that?" Jo asked.

"Funny thing. There is no report. I talked to someone I know at the lab, but they couldn't find anything. Somehow, it seems to have disappeared."

"Thorne."

"He has people everywhere." The thought made Sam nervous. Where else had Thorne placed his people? "Look, I wouldn't worry too much. I won't let you get into trouble. You haven't done anything."

Jo turned, her face screwed up in a frown. "Well, I did forge the logbook so it would look like Tyler had written in that stop. And I don't need anyone covering for me. I take responsibility for my actions."

Sam should have known better than to expect Jo to let him take the blame. "What I meant is that no one is going to know you wrote in the logbook. I don't think that will even come into the picture, and if it does, he did make the stop. His body was found there. No one will scrutinize that logbook."

"Yeah. He made the stop, but apparently not for the reasons we thought."

When Tyler's body had been found, they'd thought he'd pulled over to help someone change a tire and stumbled across a drug deal. The car with the flat tire was still at the side of the road. They'd found drug residue in the ashtray and a partial fingerprint. They'd never been able to trace that fingerprint to anyone. Now it looked as if Tyler had been up to something else entirely, although Sam had no idea what.

"What do you think he was doing out there that night?" Jo asked.

"Who knows? Maybe meeting with his contact."

"But then why was he killed? Why was the car left there with a flat tire? Sounds like a setup to me. Do you think maybe he knew too much and Thorne wanted to get rid of him? His own son?"

"Good question. Maybe there's a rival drug gang, and that's who killed Tyler. If Tyler was working with Thorne, a rival gang might have wanted to get rid of him."

Jo plopped down on the couch again and grabbed her beer. "Well, either way, it doesn't bode well for us. Especially for *you,* with that donation from the Fallen Officers Fund you gave to his mother."

Sam grimaced. Tyler had supported his mother and his disabled sister. When Tyler had died, Sam had written a check out of his retirement plan to Tyler's mother, pretending that it was a donation from the Fallen Officers Fund. Of course, that was before Sam and Jo had discovered a large deposit in Tyler's bank account. His mother had thought that deposit was back pay, but now Sam knew better. Either way, if people started looking into Tyler and discovered Sam had written a check to his mother, it could be trouble.

"What's done is done. We can't go back and change it. All we can do is damage control now," Sam said. "I wonder about Tyler's mother and Thorne, though. I can't quite picture that."

Jo raised a brow. "I know, right? You never know. That was a long time ago. Maybe Thorne was nicer then. I wonder if Tyler knew that Thorne was his real father all along or how he even found out. Seems like Thorne must have doubted it if they needed DNA testing." She shrugged and took another swig. "So how do you propose we do damage control?"

"First, we want to make sure we control the aspects of the investigation that might expose anything that could be misunderstood as wrongdoing on our part."

"Like moving the gun at the crime scene?"

"Yeah. That wasn't good judgment, but I don't think anyone needs to know I moved it. Like you said, the killer could have done it."

"I think we can probably get Kevin and Wyatt on

board with keeping quiet about anything that sheds a negative light on Tyler's reputation. As long as it's not pivotal to the investigation of Dupont's murder, I think we may be okay."

"Right. And how could it be pivotal? Tyler's been dead for months. The two are unrelated."

Jo looked thoughtful. "But we never did find out what that key locks."

They'd found a key taped under Tyler's desk after his death. They'd suspected Tyler had been up to something, though they thought he was conducting some sort of investigation on his own, never realizing that the investigation included spying on *them* for his father. They'd looked at all the safety deposit boxes and gym lockers in the area to see if the key fit but never found a match. Back then, they were hoping to get evidence on Thorne. Now, they needed to find what the key unlocked for another reason: whatever it was might contain evidence on *them*.

But what evidence? They hadn't really done anything wrong. Cut a few corners here and there. Sam didn't trust Thorne, though. For all he knew, Thorne had Tyler set things up so it looked as if they'd been doing something wrong.

"Yeah. We need to keep looking even more now. I always thought it was odd that Tyler wouldn't have included us in any off-the-book investigating he was doing. Now we know why."

"There's another wrinkle that we need to watch out for," Jo said. "Mick was at the crime scene that night. What if someone saw him leaving?"

"I thought about that. Let's hope no one saw him. If it comes up, we'll have to handle it."

Mick Gervasi was Sam's best friend, his buddy since grade school, and a private investigator that he often hired to look into things when Sam couldn't do it officially. They'd had Mick investigating Tyler when they'd been told it was a conflict for them to investigate. He'd made little headway other than to discover that the car that had been left at the crime scene had been stolen. Mick suspected the grandson of the car's owner had something to do with that theft.

Sam drained his beer. "You want another?"

Jo held hers up to the light, barely a half inch of liquid swirling in the bottom of the bottle. "Why not? It's not like I'll get pulled over on the way home."

Sam got up to grab the beer from the refrigerator. Jo walked around the cabin, stopping in front of a birch-framed photo of Sam's twin daughters, Hayley and Marla. Sam remembered taking that photo on a ski trip a few years ago.

"How are the girls?"

Sam's heart swelled with thoughts of his daughters. They were the only good things that had come of his first marriage. They were both in college, pursuing careers in Massachusetts. Sam missed them. He wanted them to come back to White Rock, but they claimed there were no opportunities up here near the Canadian border for ambitious young women.

Still, he harbored a glimmer of hope that someday, when they were older, they'd realize nothing compared to the beauty of the mountains and the laid-back lifestyle. If Thorne didn't ruin it before then.

"They're doing pretty well." Sam popped the tops off both beers and handed one to Jo. "Marla is doing an internship at Woods Hole, and Hayley is taking some summer classes to try to speed up that pharmacology degree."

"Nice girls," Jo said. When Jo had first come on board, the girls had been in high school. Sam was under no illusions that his girls were angels. He knew they got into the same sort of trouble he had as a teen. Nothing big. Drinking. Boys. He also knew that Jo had cut them some slack on a few occasions, even though she and the twins thought they were keeping it from him.

Jo sipped her beer and looked at him hesitantly.

Sam wondered why. She could tell him anything. "Something on your mind?"

"The knife. We never found it."

Sam sighed. The knife had been on his mind too. It all went back to Sam's cousin, Gracie. She'd been raped in Boston decades ago. Sam and Mick had been young then, Sam just starting out in law enforcement. The rapists were from wealthy families, and not all of them got the punishment they deserved. Sam and Mick had taken matters into their own hands to try to force the truth to come out so there could be justice for Gracie. Things hadn't worked out exactly as they'd planned.

Somehow, Dupont knew something about what had happened back then. He hadn't been involved in the rape, but he must have known the players. And Dupont had never been one to pass up an opportunity to get something to hold over someone else's head. He'd come into possession of Mick's pocketknife, which had been left in a place it shouldn't have. He'd passed it along to Thorne. And now Thorne was using it to threaten Sam. If that knife made its way to the police, things might not look too good for Mick.

Sam and Mick had shared some of this with Jo the night they'd found Dupont. In a way, it had felt good telling her. Keeping the secret had weighed heavily on

Sam, as if it were something between them. But now it burdened Jo just as much. He almost wished he'd never told her.

"Let's not worry about that now. That problem will be solved once we prove that Thorne is behind this murder and we put him away."

"I guess you're right." Jo didn't seem convinced, and Sam had the feeling there was something more she wanted to say. He could see indecision in her face, but then she smiled, and Sam thought maybe he'd imagined it. "Don't worry. We'll nail him, and everything will work out, especially now that we have another cop to help out."

"What do you think of the new guy?" Sam asked. They stood in the kitchen now. Sam glanced out at the backyard and the cedar doghouse he'd built for Lucy a few weeks ago. She never used it because she was always by his side, but he felt better knowing she had shelter if she wanted to go outside. Sam leaned his hip against the counter, and Jo leaned her shoulder against the large cedar log that anchored the built-in bookshelves between the kitchen and the living room.

Her forehead creased slightly. "I'm not sure what to make of him yet. I haven't worked with him very much. He seems a little cautious."

Sam nodded. He hadn't really formed an opinion

of Wyatt yet, either, but he sensed there was more to the guy. He had the disconcerting feeling that Wyatt was watching him, as if waiting for something to happen. Maybe he was only trying to figure out where he stood in the department and what Sam was about. It would take a while for him to get a good bead on Wyatt.

"So, what do we do next?" Jo asked.

Sam swigged his beer. "Run it like any other homicide. This one's actually easier. We already know who's at the bottom of it. We just need to get the facts to prove it."

CHAPTER SIX

The stress rolled off of Jo's shoulders as soon as she pulled up in front of the small cottage in the woods that she called home. She loved the remote location, away from the hustle and bustle—not that White Rock had much hustle or bustle, for that matter. Jo liked the seclusion, liked not being able to see her neighbors, the serenity of being in the woods with nothing but birds and the brook beyond the cottage to interrupt her thoughts.

The sun had set, and she could hear the cicadas buzzing as she headed up the steps of the front porch. Beyond the cottage, the flickering of fireflies at the edge of the dark woods gave the scene a magical feel.

On the porch, she stuck her finger into one of the

railing boxes overflowing with bright-red petunias. They were looking a little wilted. Yep, the soil was dry. She'd been putting in so many hours on the Dupont case and the stakeout she'd neglected her flowers. She made a mental note to water them early the next morning.

She glanced down at the empty bowl beside the door. She'd seen an orange cat out back a few times and had been putting food out for him. She didn't know if he had a home or not, but he looked pretty thin. Maybe eventually she'd make friends with him. Maybe even adopt him. Was she ready for that kind of commitment?

The interior of the cottage was cozy. Jo liked the freshness of the off-white and pale florals she decorated in. The chippy paint she'd applied to update her furniture had turned her shabby yard sale finds into chic retro pieces. The cottage was small, but her needs were simple.

She had never planned to stay in White Rock. She'd come for a specific reason. But now that reason didn't seem so important. She loved her job, and she loved working with Sam. And much to her dismay, she discovered that she wanted to stay in White Rock.

At first when she'd come, she hadn't put any time

into decorating the cottage because she thought she wouldn't stay. But it had been a few years, and things had crept in. Yard sale finds, flea market treasures. Now she had it exactly as she wanted, comfortable and cozy. The cottage had become the home she never knew she wanted.

She'd even gotten a pet. Finn wasn't a furry, cuddly pet like Lucy; he was a goldfish. A fish had been about all she could handle in the way of commitment.

Her eyes darted to the aquarium in the corner. Finn swam around, his orange-gold scales shimmering in the fluorescent tank lighting as he darted under the ceramic bridge then past the treasure chest that opened, sending bubbles rising to the top, before weaving around several aquatic plants in the corner.

She carefully plucked one large flake of food from the fish food container. She'd been training Finn to take food from her hand. She opened the lid and poised the flake just above the surface of the water. Finn swam up. His golden eyes looked up at her, his lips broke the surface, and he grabbed the flake before swimming down under his bridge. Odd—he usually stayed at the surface longer.

"What's the matter, guy?"

Maybe he was lonely. Jo was a little lonely too. Maybe she should get a bigger pet, something that could sit in her lap. The few times Sam had come over with Lucy, it had felt good to have a dog in her cottage. It had seemed right. Now that she was sure she was staying, a pet could be the thing. The next step on the road to commitment. Not a dog, though. That was too big a step. Maybe a cat, like the stray out back. But she couldn't have a pet in her cottage. She was just renting. Perhaps now was the time to buy a place.

With Finn fed, her eyes turned to the bedroom, and a familiar ominous feeling settled in. The room was decorated like the rest of the house. White chenille bedspread on a queen-sized bed, the headboard of which was an old fireplace mantel painted off-white. In the corner, a gigantic robin's-egg blue armoire sat, the sight of which speared Jo with a pang of guilt.

Inside the armoire was the real reason she'd come to White Rock. A reason she'd never told Sam about. And now that Sam had shared his secret about his cousin and the knife, Jo felt that she should share hers. But the time had never been right, and now she thought that perhaps it was time to give up on the investigation that had haunted her most of her life. Somehow, it didn't seem important to her anymore. It was time to move on.

She lifted the corner of the rug at the foot of her bed and grabbed the brass skeleton key that opened the armoire. The armoire was her workstation. Inside, her laptop sat on a shelf in the middle. The insides of the doors were covered with notes and photos on the two cases she was working.

One of those cases was Tyler's. The other—the one that had been her obsession—was the case of her sister. Looking at the yellowed photos tacked inside the armoire door twisted Jo's heart. She still mourned Tammy, who had been abducted when they were children thirty years ago. She'd never been found, and it had ripped Jo's family apart. No wonder she had commitment problems.

The police had stopped looking after the case grew cold. Years later, when a female serial killer had been caught, the cops thought she'd been the one behind Jo's sister's disappearance. But the killer denied it. Jo had at least hoped she could tell her where her sister's body was. The finality of a body would be difficult, but it would bring closure.

The cops said the killer might be holding back to use those last unclosed cases as leverage somehow. Jo wasn't so sure. And that was why she'd become a cop and had been looking into the case herself all these years. She'd been led to White Rock when she'd heard rumors of a copycat killer in the area. But those rumors had been unfounded, and no killer ever surfaced.

Her sister's disappearance had eaten away at her for years, but somehow, coming to White Rock had been cathartic. She'd found herself thinking less and less about solving her sister's case and more about solving the cases that affected her new town.

Maybe now, after all these years, it was time to put her sister's case to rest. Time to heal her old wounds and move on. And if she let go of her sister's case, she wouldn't have that secret. She'd never have to tell Sam about the real reason she'd hired on here.

Jo's focus turned to the right side of the armoire, where she kept her notes and research on Tyler's case. Here she had been, trying to find Tyler's killer, and it turned out he had been screwing them over. She stifled the urge to rip all the notes and photos down and tear them to pieces. They still needed to find the box that key opened, and her notes might help. Now more than ever, she was afraid of what might be inside.

She turned back to the left side and carefully removed the photos, some of them brittle and yellow with age. Over the years, she'd collected whatever she could from the detectives who had originally investigated the case. She had notebooks filled with notes, all of which led nowhere.

She placed the photographs in a manila envelope, her gaze falling on one black and white of several shallow graves. That photo had haunted her dreams almost every night. Her sister was in a grave just like that, still waiting to be discovered and brought back home.

The graves all had something in common. They were all near beech trees that had some of the lower branches broken. When Jo had pointed this out to the officers who had investigated, they shrugged it off. They said she was trying to read things into the case that weren't there. The case had been twenty years old by then. The original investigators had retired. No one really cared about an old cold case in which they thought they'd already incarcerated the killer.

Maybe they were right. Maybe, in her desperation to solve the case, she had been reading too much into the trees. It wasn't uncommon for branches to break, especially with the harsh New England winters. Besides, she'd been all over the woods here in White Rock and never found any indication of unmarked graves near beech trees.

She slowly put the rest of the photographs in the folder then piled it on top of the notebooks. She opened the bottom drawer, took out several layers of folded jeans, and placed the folder and notebooks on the bottom before putting the jeans on top.

It was time to move on. It was time to start anew and focus on putting Thorne away so that she could clean up the town she intended to call her home for the rest of her life.

CHAPTER SEVEN

"I've got good news and bad news," Reese said the next morning as she came around the post office boxes into the squad room where Sam, Jo, Kevin, and Wyatt were going over the case. She held up a white bag from Brewed Awakening. "And doughnuts. Harry dropped them off."

As she handed the bag to Jo, Sam glanced toward the lobby, expecting to see Harry, but he wasn't there. Apparently, he'd dropped off the treats and left. Maybe he wasn't so annoying after all.

"What's the good news?" Sam asked as Jo passed him the bag of doughnuts. At his feet, Lucy's ears whipped to attention at the sound of the bag opening.

"We've got a partial on that fingerprint from the

leaf that Kevin bagged," Reese said. "Turns out it is a print."

Kevin pulled a cruller from the bag. "Really? Did you get a match?"

"No match."

"So, that's the bad news, then," Jo said.

"Not quite." The bag came back around to Reese. She ripped off a tiny piece of a glazed doughnut and chewed it thoughtfully. "This might be good news or bad news, I'm not sure, but that partial print did match something."

"What?"

"Matches the one found in the car that was left at the scene when Tyler was shot," she mumbled while munching.

Sam exchanged a glance with Jo. This was a new wrinkle, but what did it mean?

"That's your officer who was killed earlier this summer?" Wyatt asked.

Sam nodded.

Wyatt leaned back in his chair, his arms crossed over his chest. "Well, what do you make of that? What do you know about the car or the circumstances? Could this have something to do with the mayor?"

"We don't know much. The state police took over the investigation pretty quickly, so we didn't get a chance to look into too much." Sam looked down at his doughnut. It was only sort of a lie. The state police *had* taken over. Sam had just left out the part about how he and Jo continued investigating on the side.

"So, his death *could* be tied to the murder of the mayor," Wyatt said.

"We think Tyler stumbled onto some drug activity the night he was killed," Kevin said.

Sam nodded. The car contained drug residue, and that was as good a theory as any, given what Kevin and Wyatt knew about Tyler. But from what Sam and Jo knew about him, his death could have been for another reason entirely. Sam decided to change the subject and keep the focus on the Dupont investigation. "Did you guys get any information from anyone who frequents the mill?"

Wyatt shrugged. "Not much. One of them did see a unicorn that night."

"And another swears angels are flying around in the rafters," Kevin said.

"Probably the pigeons," Jo said.

"Right. I'm afraid we won't get much from any of them. Not only are they hard to find because most of them seem to be homeless or get shuffled between friends and relatives, but anything they say isn't really that reliable," Wyatt said.

"I didn't figure we'd get much, but we have to follow every lead. I was hoping one of them might lead us to whoever sold them drugs. Then we could find out where he gets them. Eventually, that chain leads to Thorne's most trusted minion, and *that's* the person who can give us the information to put Thorne away." Sam glanced at the investigation photos tacked to the corkboard identical to the one in his office. "I have a few other ideas on how we can get that information."

"I know you guys are focusing on the Dupont case, but I did get some other calls this morning," Reese said. "Wyatt must have made an impression on Rita. She's requesting he come out and solve a dispute. Nettie has retaliated with a claim that Rita's chicken flew over the fence and ate all Bitsy's food. And Hank O'Brien claims Bullwinkle ate his wife's petunias and she's running around in their backyard in her bathrobe with a shotgun, ready to shoot him."

Sam blew out a breath. "We'd better get on that one. Her aim isn't too good. Might hit the neighbor."

White Rock and the surrounding region hosted a healthy population of moose, some of which occasionally strolled into town. The locals thought it was one moose in particular that they'd named Bullwinkle. He even had a Facebook page where residents posted sightings.

Now Sam was glad they'd hired Wyatt. They couldn't ignore the local calls even with the ongoing murder investigation. Having another cop would help Sam and Jo to maintain focus on the murder.

"Okay, Kevin, you take Hank, and then clock out when you're done." Kevin was still part-time and had come in early to read water meters on South Main Street. In a small town, the police were called upon for other duties, and in White Rock, that meant reading meters. "Wyatt, looks like you're up for Rita."

Wyatt and Kevin got up to leave just as the lobby door swung open. Everyone turned toward the post office boxes. Sam figured Harry was making his return. Maybe he'd gone back to Brewed Awakening to get coffee for everyone. Sam certainly hoped so; the shop's coffee was a lot better than the K-Cups. But Sam was disappointed.

It wasn't Harry with coffee. It was Henley Jamison with a load of arrogance.

Jamison had a scowl on his pretty-boy face that made Sam want to punch him. "Good to see White Rock's finest at work."

Lucy let out a soft growl, and Sam tossed her part of a doughnut. She wolfed it down as she continued to eye Jamison warily.

Jamison didn't wait for a reply. "I just got off the

phone with John Dudley. He's sure Dupont was murdered. I want this solved pronto. We can't have a killer running around White Rock. When word gets out the mayor was murdered, people will be nervous. That's bad for tourism dollars, and that might not bode well for me getting elected mayor. We need a quick conviction."

In Sam's opinion, making things look good for Jamison was a reason to *not* solve the murder quickly. He was the last person Sam wanted as mayor. But he wouldn't stall the case because of that.

Sam gestured to the corkboard. "We're working on it."

Jamison straightened his red silk tie. "That's all well and good, but I'm not sure you can solve this on your own."

Jo scoffed. "Sure we can. We've solved three homicides already this summer."

Jamison frowned as if he wasn't used to people talking back to him. "This is a high-profile case, and there are only two seasoned full-time officers here. One is part-time, and another is new. I don't want it to look as if I shirked my duties in providing the best resources. There's a killer running loose."

So that was what it was about: Jamison's reputation with the voters. Not about finding the killer. Sam wasn't surprised.

"I think we can do the job," Sam said. He didn't want to argue too forcefully about keeping the investigation to themselves because that might look suspicious. Better to play along and be wary of whoever Jamison sent in to help. "We appreciate the offer, but we don't need the help."

"I'm afraid it's not negotiable."

The doughnut bag crinkled loudly as Jo's fist crushed it into a ball. Sam tensed, fearing she was about to throw it at Jamison.

Lucy looked up at her hopefully.

Jamison frowned at her fist. "I'm bringing in the county sheriff, Bev Hatch. She'll be here this afternoon for a briefing."

Jamison pivoted on his heel and strode out.

Sam glanced at the others. Wyatt looked mildly amused. Jo looked pissed. Kevin looked thoughtful.

"Damn, I hate it when outsiders come in," Kevin said.

"I know Bev," Sam said. "She's a straight shooter, and I don't think she's corrupt. Maybe this will be a good thing. We really could use the extra help."

"I don't see how. Whenever someone new comes in, they mess things up," Jo said.

"All the more reason to get this solved quickly. I have an idea where to start," Sam said. "We need to find whoever is working closest with Thorne, and because there're very few clues to go on at the crime scene, I'm going to start working my way up the ladder. I have an informant I've been cultivating just for this. I think it's time to pay him a visit."

CHAPTER EIGHT

Kevin and Wyatt took off, Kevin using the Crown Vic, Wyatt using his own car. Sam and Jo hopped into the Tahoe with Lucy in back.

"So what do you make of this fingerprint?" Jo asked as Sam pulled away from the curb and headed down Main Street toward the rolling layers of blue mountains in the distance.

"Not sure. We already know Tyler was mixed up with Thorne, so his death probably was the result of a drug deal gone bad. And the fingerprint belongs to someone within Thorne's drug organization."

"But who? If Tyler was *with* the bad guys on the side of the road that night, who shot him?"

Sam shrugged. "More bad guys?"

It was a puzzle. If Tyler had been working with

Thorne and the blown tire was a setup, who set him up? Did Thorne have enemies Sam didn't know about? And if so, did they have something to do with Dupont's death? Sam wasn't keen on the thought that he might get rid of Thorne only to have someone worse take his place.

"You don't think Thorne wanted to get rid of Tyler, do you?" Jo asked.

"His own son?" The thought was abhorrent to Sam. He would jump in front of a bullet for his daughters, but Thorne was a different kind of man. "I guess he doesn't seem to be much of a family man."

"Yeah, he's mean. Doesn't seem to care much about anyone but himself. Though I find it funny that he's afraid of his wife, at least according to Harry," Jo said.

"This fingerprint could be a bonus for us. If we find who the print belongs to, we might be able to solve both Tyler's case and Dupont's case and get what we need on Thorne."

"*If.*" Jo pressed her lips together and looked out the passenger window. "So I take it we're going to visit Jesse."

"Yep." Sam hadn't had to name his informant. She knew it was Jesse Cowly, a small-time pot dealer who sold mostly to his friends and used the money to finance his own supply. Sam had been cultivating him for a while, overlooking minor infractions and looking the other way when he caught Jesse with pot. He'd been trying to build a relationship, gain his confidence, and get into a position in which Jesse owed him some favors. Now it was time to collect.

"Good, then we can stop at Brewed Awakening." Jo pointed toward the gigantic coffee cup sign of their favorite drive-through.

"Glad you said that." Sam pulled in. "The coffee at the station is okay, but I need something stronger today."

"So you're thinking we'll find out who Jesse gets his drugs from, then find out where that guy gets his drugs from, and eventually that leads us to the top of the chain," Jo said after Sam ordered the coffees and a doughnut hole for Lucy.

"I don't think we're going to have to go too far up. This isn't New York City, so Thorne probably has only one or two guys between him and the dirty work. Whoever is closest to Thorne probably knows who killed Dupont. Might even be the killer. Either way, the higher-ups will know enough about Thorne's operation to put him in jail." Sam took the order, flipped Lucy a small bite of doughnut, and handed Jo her coffee.

Jo flipped the lid on her coffee and took a sip. "That Jamison really is a piece of work, huh?"

"Yeah, I would have thought with Dupont gone, things would get easier, but it turns out Jamison might be even worse. Thankfully, we only have to suffer with him until next fall."

"What do you think of Marnie Wilson?" Jo's voice had an odd tone, and Sam looked over to see her peering at him over the top of her police-issue Oakleys. He got the weird feeling the question had a double meaning, but darned if he could figure out what it was.

"Well, anyone's better than Jamison or Dupont," Sam said.

Marnie Wilson was running for mayor. She had the vote of most of the seniors in town, who were sick of all the building Thorne was doing. He'd been systematically buying out farms when the elderly owners died off, and now, instead of rolling fields and mountain views, the town was turning into hotels and parking lots.

"Harry seems to think she's taken a shine to you." Jo sipped her coffee with a smirk. "Just sayin'."

Sam looked at her out of the corner of his eye. Was she joking? Sam vaguely remembered Harry saying something like that, but he hadn't thought of Marnie in that way. Heck, he'd met her only once. Though he supposed she was attractive in an authoritative sort of way, Sam had more important things on his mind.

"What do you think about Jamison bringing in the sheriff? This could be bad for us, you know, considering everything with Tyler."

"Might not be. I know Bev a little. She's a straight shooter, like I said, and we're not doing anything wrong. We're working this just like a homicide."

"I know, but what if ..."

"Nothing's gonna happen. I'm sure Bev is busy with her own cases. She probably doesn't have much time to spend on this. And she doesn't answer to Jamison, so she can tell him to shove it if he tries to impede progress as Dupont used to do. That could work in our favor."

"I suppose." Jo shifted in her seat to look out the passenger window. "Hey, there's Bullwinkle. Or one of them." Jo pointed down a side street where a giant bull moose meandered toward the wooded area at the end. Someone was snapping off a photo with their cell phone.

"That'll be up on the Facebook page later today," Sam said. "I'm just glad Mrs. O'Brien isn't running after him in her bathrobe with a shotgun."

Jo snorted as Sam turned onto the dirt road that led to Jesse's small ranch house near the town line. A few minutes later, they pulled up to the house. The grass—or at least the patches of grass that could be seen in the predominantly dirt front yard—had been mowed. The torn edge of the screen on the door that had flapped open the last time he'd been there had been repaired. Maybe Jesse was cleaning up his act. Sam hoped not; he was useful as an informant.

They got out, and Lucy trotted ahead of them to the door, her nose in the air. She'd been here with them more than once, and the place usually smelled like pot. She was probably already sniffing it out.

Jesse answered the door, a wary look on his face. He held up his hands. "I don't know anything about the mayor."

"Can we come in?" Sam asked.

Jesse glanced out into the street nervously. Even though the road didn't have any traffic and the next neighbor was a good distance away, Sam knew he didn't want to be seen inviting the cops into his house.

Apparently satisfied no one was looking, Jesse opened the screen door and gestured for them to enter the living room.

Lucy's nose twitched rapidly at the smorgasbord of smells inside the house. A pizza box lay open on the coffee table, and the smell of stale cheese and marinara still hung in the air. Dirty socks were strewn about the floor.

"Where's your roommate?" Jesse lived with his cousin Brian. Sam hoped that Brian was at work. He wanted the conversation to be private.

"At work." Jesse stood off to the side, his arms across his chest. Sam sauntered to the coffee table, where Lucy had honed in on a black-lacquer-lidded box that sat in the middle. Sam guessed the box housed Jesse's latest stash.

"We know you didn't have anything to do with the mayor," Sam said as he tilted his head to look at the box from an angle. "But we're hoping you might be able to help us figure out who did."

"How?" Jesse sidled over to the coffee table and nonchalantly picked up the box and then placed it on top of the entertainment center, out of Lucy's reach.

"We need to know who you get your drugs from."

"What?" Jesse scrubbed twitchy hands through his hair. "I can't tell you that."

"Sure you can." Sam stepped closer to Jesse. "Because if you don't, you might end up in jail, and then there might be a rumor that you did tell me whether you did or not."

Sam held Jesse's gaze long enough to see the fear and anger cross his eyes before Jesse's gaze dropped to the floor. He sighed. "Okay. Well, I don't know the top guy who reports to Thorne. It's a chain of command."

"I know," Sam said. "I only want to know the next guy up the chain. I'll figure it out from there. Normally, I wouldn't do this, Jesse, but it could help us solve two murders. I know you don't want your drug supply to dry up, but I need to know who you get it from. I'm gonna find out one way or the other."

Jesse crossed his arms over his chest. "I don't know the top dog. There're layers."

"Yeah, I get that. Just spill it. We won't let on that it came from you."

Jesse looked at them uncertainly, but he must have realized Sam wasn't messing around. And because Sam hadn't busted him before, they had a bit of trust between them. Finally, he relented.

"Okay, fine. It's Scott Elliott. I get my stuff from him," Jesse said.

"You know where he lives?" Sam asked.

"Over near that new pharmacy, I think. He keeps the business away from his house."

"Smart," Jo said as they turned to leave.

"Come to think of it, I did hear something that might help you."

Sam turned back, his brows raised.

"Like I said, Scott doesn't do any deals at his house.

We meet here and there. Sometimes it's hard to find a place."

"I imagine," Jo said.

"But Scott once said something about the guy he gets the stuff from having the perfect day job for delivering drugs."

"What do you mean, like a UPS guy or something?" Jo asked.

Jesse pressed his lips together. "Maybe, but I got the impression it was someone with ties to the government."

"You mean someone who works at the town hall here?" Sam frowned, conjuring up the faces and roles of the people who worked in the brick building that served as town hall. The only sketchy one he could come up with was Jamison.

"More like someone who would have an excuse to be seen all around town." Jesse raised his brows. "You know, like a cop."

CHAPTER NINE

B ack in the Tahoe, Jo looked up Scott Elliott on her iPad. "Elliott lives on Hawthorne Street. We should get over there right away before he skips town."

"Can't." Sam pointed at the digital clock on the dash. "Bev Hatch is due at the station any minute."

Jo sighed, sank back in her seat, and pushed her Oakleys up on her nose. She wasn't sure what to think about Bev Hatch. She glanced at Sam. He didn't seem nervous at all. After working with him for so long, she knew the telltale signs—the tightening of his jaw, the tic in his cheek. If Sam wasn't nervous about Bev, maybe she shouldn't be either.

But there was one thing that did make her nervous, and she was pretty sure it made Sam nervous, too. "What did Jesse mean that the distributor could be a cop?" she asked. "Do you think that's part of Thorne's plan to frame us?"

"Maybe. That would get us out of the way. He could put in his own people."

"He already had his own person in there: Tyler."

"Yeah, and Tyler's not there anymore. Maybe he needs to get someone new into place, and in order to do that, he'd have to get rid of me."

Jo frowned. She didn't like the idea of anyone getting rid of Sam. "Well, I won't let that happen."

Sam smiled but kept his eyes on the road.

"But it could be any government employee. Might not be a cop. We might just be paranoid. Jesse probably just said 'cops' to get us riled up."

"Yeah, it could be any government employee, like Jamison." Jo tapped her finger on her thigh as she thought the idea through. "You know, he's been dying to get the mayor position. I heard rumors he was thinking of running against Dupont. Now, Dupont's gone, and nothing stands in his way."

"Not exactly. He has the position until the election, but he has to beat Marnie Wilson to keep it." Sam pressed his lips together. "But now that you mention it, no one else has thrown their hat in the ring. I can't picture Jamison getting his Ferragamo shoes dirty with murder, though."

"It doesn't necessarily have to be someone who works here in town. It could be someone who works for the county," Jo said. "Like, maybe Bev Hatch. Jamison seemed pretty keen to bring her in on this. Maybe they're in on it together."

Sam thought for a minute and then shook his head. "I don't think so. Bev's been sheriff for a long time, and I've never heard of her being corrupt. My grandpa knew her family." He shrugged as he pulled onto Main Street. "Then again, you never know who you can trust."

"Well, we know we can trust ourselves." Jo glanced into the backseat, where Lucy sat happily looking out the window. "And Lucy."

They pulled up in front of the police station to see the Coos County Sheriff car parked in front.

"At least Hatch is on time. I hate when these sheriffs get on a power trip and purposely show up late so you have to wait for them," Jo said as they piled out of the SUV and followed Lucy into the station.

Bev Hatch was short and in her midfifties, with shoulder-length salt-and-pepper hair pulled back in a simple ponytail. Her piercing gray eyes read "no nonsense," and Jo got the impression that Bev had sized her up in the first two seconds she'd laid eyes on her. Jo wasn't sure what her conclusions were, but when Bev's eyes fell on Lucy, a smile lit her face, and she earned a few points with Jo.

Bev pulled a dog treat from her pocket and squatted to Lucy's eye level. "Heard about you, Miss Lucy. You're quite the K-9 cop."

Lucy sniffed Bev's hand, swished her tail back and forth, and took the treat.

Bev stood and introduced herself to Jo, shaking her hand, and then shook Sam's. "Nice to see you again, Sam."

"Same here."

Bev looked around and nodded. "Nice place you got here. I like an old-fashioned police station. So, why don't you fill me in on what you've got so far?"

The three of them stood in front of the corkboard as Sam told Bev everything they knew about the investigation. Bev had already seen the crime scene photos, and they discussed a few of the details. They brought her up to speed on the fingerprint Kevin found and what they'd learned from Jesse.

Bev's eyes narrowed when Sam told her the fingerprint matched the one found on the car at Tyler's shooting.

"That's an odd coincidence. By the way, I'm really sorry about your loss." Bev's eyes drifted to the desk in the corner. Wyatt hadn't yet had a chance to clutter it up, and it was still so empty that it obviously used to be Tyler's. "Weird they never caught the guy and now the matching print turns up. I don't think that's any coincidence, do you?"

"Probably not," Sam said.

"Was Tyler investigating anything to do with the mayor?" Bev asked.

"Not that I'm aware of, but he might have stumbled onto something that night. I was going on the idea that it was some kind of drug deal."

Bev's gaze returned to the corkboard. "Why do you think the killer ran out through the woods? Do you think he could have been one of the vagrants squatting in the mill? Maybe Dupont's arrival surprised them. You know, if they were high, anything could happen."

"That's a thought, but how do you explain the gun? Most of these vagrants don't carry guns."

Bev nodded. "*Most* of them don't. Some do. The serial number was filed off. Sent it up to the big lab in Concord. They can do more forensics on it than we can at the county lab." Bev's clipped tone showed that she was fast and efficient.

"But why *leave* the gun?"

Bev shrugged. "Ya got me. Why do *you* think they left it? And why did the person who killed Dupont wear gloves, but the person who ran through the woods didn't?"

"Maybe the person who ran through the woods had nothing to do with the murder. Maybe they happened across the scene after, got scared, and ran," Sam suggested.

Bev pressed her lips together. "You know, that would explain something. John Dudley told me it looked as though the mayor had been patted down—as if somebody was looking for something."

Jo's gut clenched, and she kept her eyes trained on the photos, trying not to show any emotion. Mick had patted Dupont down, looking for the knife. Unfortunately, they hadn't found it.

"Possibly one of the vagrants or drug users looking for money," Sam said. "Dupont must have gotten there early, because when we got to the mill, the blood was already starting to dry. He'd been killed about a half hour before we got there."

Bev frowned. "Now, why do you think he got there early?"

"Maybe he wanted to scout out the mill and make sure we were coming alone." Sam shrugged. "Maybe he was meeting with someone else before us. Who knows?"

Bev crossed her arms over her chest and leaned a

hip against the desk. "Now tell me about this meeting. Dupont was supposed to give you incriminating information on the drug situation here in town. Is that right?"

Sam nodded. "Dupont was going to give us evidence on Lucas Thorne."

Bev's left brow ticked up. "The real estate developer? Interesting. I'd heard rumors he was into something shady. Never liked that guy. Bit of a pompous ass."

"You can say that again," Jo said, earning a slight smile from Bev.

"We never got the evidence because Dupont was dead when we got there," Sam said.

"Seems like Thorne would have good motive to kill him," Bev said. She seemed to consider this hunch carefully. And Jo's confidence grew. She got the impression that Bev was sharp, and she didn't seem to be pushing the investigation in any one direction. She was taking the information at face value. Maybe Sam was right and things wouldn't be so bad.

"One possibility is that someone left the gun to frame someone else," Jo said.

"Who?" Bev asked.

"Possibly us," Sam said. "My contact, Jesse, told us that the rumor was that the head of drug distribution was some sort of municipal employee. He specifically mentioned it could be a cop."

"And you think Thorne is arranging to frame you to get you out of the way."

Sam nodded.

"Lucky I can tell the difference between planted evidence and real evidence," Bev said.

Somehow, Bev's words didn't make Jo feel better. It would be great if she wasn't fooled by anything that Thorne had planted, but that also meant she might be able to smell a rat about some of the things that Sam and she had done.

"So, you have two other officers working on this, but one is only part-time." Bev looked around the squad room at the three desks.

"That's correct," Sam said.

"That's not much manpower. Unfortunately, I don't have a lot of extra manpower myself. But we'll try to do what we can. That Jamison is no prize to deal with, either, but the murder of a mayor is serious. If your hunch about Thorne is correct, this is a big case. It needs to be done right."

"I agree," Sam said, "especially if one of us is being framed."

Bev pursed her lips and nodded solemnly just as the door to the lobby opened and Wyatt entered.

Sam introduced Wyatt to Bev.

"Did you settle things down with Rita and Nettie?" Sam asked Wyatt before turning to Bev and explaining, "Bit of a local dispute this morning. Still have to handle those too."

Bev nodded as if she was all too familiar with having to juggle petty disputes and bigger investigations.

"I got things settled." Wyatt held up a loaf-shaped package wrapped in pink cellophane. "Rita sent you a fruitcake."

Sam took the fruitcake, a frown on his face. He looked down at Lucy. Lucy sniffed the air, disinterested, apparently deciding she wasn't a fan of fruitcake. She turned and trotted to her plush dog bed and flopped down.

"I might have gotten a tip on the Dupont case from Rita," Wyatt said.

"Really?"

"She said she was walking Bitsy down the access road to the mill. I guess there's a path that intersects with it in the woods near her house. She can see the access road from the path. Anyway, she said she saw an SUV racing out of there right after she heard the police sirens."

Jo's gut clenched. An SUV? That would have been

Mick's.

Bev's interest was piqued. "What kind of SUV? Could she identify it?"

"She just said it was a black SUV. With roof racks." Wyatt grimaced. "I tried to get her to be more specific, but she said she can't see that well and she doesn't know the makes."

Bev looked at Sam. "We should have her in. Maybe we can show her photos of black SUVs to help her identify the model. I want to interview her."

"Yes, we should do that," Sam said. "But Rita's elderly and a local. I want to be there because she'll get nervous. I don't want her to be afraid."

"I understand that. I have locals in my county too." Bev pressed her lips together and looked out the window. "But one thing's odd. If the killer drove away in an SUV, how could he leave a fingerprint while running through the woods?"

"And why would Rita have seen the SUV after hearing the sirens?" Wyatt turned to Sam and Jo. "Dupont had already been dead for a while when you got to the mill, right? I assume the killer would have been long gone."

"Would seem that way," Sam said. "But maybe he wasn't. Maybe he was in there, doing something, and we scared him off. John did say it looked as if someone had gone through Dupont's pockets. If this was Thorne's doing, he might have instructed the killer to look for incriminating evidence."

"We called it in right away, so the timeline would make sense," Jo added.

"Didn't you hear a vehicle driving off?" Bev asked.

Jo exchanged a glance with Sam. "No. Well, tell the truth, it was kind of loud with all the pigeons flapping around in there. And we didn't see an SUV, but if it was parked down the road in the woods, we wouldn't have seen it, and the sound of the engine would have been barely audible inside the mill." Great, now she was thinking up lies off the cuff and telling them to the county sheriff.

Wyatt glanced at the corkboard. "So the SUV that Rita saw could be the killer's?"

"Most likely." Bev looked at Sam. "Is there any other reason someone would be out there? Another building or someone's home?"

"There're walking trails out there. Someone could have parked to use the trails and just happened to be leaving at that time," Sam said.

"Either way, it would be good to find this person. If not the killer, they might have seen something."

"I'll do a search of all the black SUVs in the area," Wyatt said.

"Good idea. I'll shoot back to my office and follow up with the lab on the gun. See if they found anything else," Bev said.

"Jo and I will check out the lead we got from Jesse," Sam said. "And I'll get Reese to call Rita to see if she can come in later this afternoon."

"Let me know what time, and I'll swing by and sit in." Bev glanced at the package wrapped in pink cellophane on Sam's desk, her nose wrinkling. "Let's just hope she doesn't bring more fruitcake."

CHAPTER TEN

Kevin arrived home from the morning shift to find a note from his contact under the mat at his back door. Damn, he was hoping the contact might have lost interest, because he hadn't heard from him in a while. No such luck.

He brought the note inside and fixed a cup of tea. His hands shook as he opened it. What would they want now? With the ongoing investigation of the mayor's murder, Kevin didn't have a good feeling about what the contact was going to ask him to do.

The words were scrawled, as if someone was trying to hide their handwriting. But the message was clear. Steer the investigation toward Sam Mason's cabin. Critical evidence under the doghouse.

Kevin burned the note and then sat contemplating

what to do. Someone was trying to frame Sam. Now he knew for sure that Sam and Jo weren't doing anything wrong. His contact had been the one working for the wrong side all along. Probably working for Thorne.

There was no way Kevin would let Sam go down for this murder. For once in his life, he had to go out on a limb and do something. He had to make up for the information he'd passed along this past year.

Kevin had an idea, but he'd have to be careful. It would mean crossing Thorne, which might result in Kevin ending up dead in a pool of blood just like Dupont. But if he played his cards right, maybe he could pull it off.

He was in a good position because he could pass information that would put off discovering whatever was under the dog house back to his contact. He could make it seem as though he was setting things up so the evidence stuck. Meanwhile, he had an idea of how he could get both him and Sam out of this and possibly get something they could use against Thorne.

He got in his car and drove to the woods near Sam's cabin. He knew Sam was at work and no one was home, but he didn't want his car seen at Sam's house. He parked on another street and took a trail through the woods that brought him near the back of Sam's property.

He stuck to the edge of the woods, following it to Sam's backyard. The doghouse that Sam had built for Lucy was at the very edge of the woods, under a stand of pine trees.

It wasn't hard to figure out where they'd buried something. Kevin got on his hands and knees and carefully scraped away the dirt from under the northwest corner of the doghouse like an archaeologist uncovering a precious artifact. But it wasn't an artifact. It was a bloody glove. Presumably one of the gloves that Dupont's killer had worn.

Kevin put on his own gloves to transfer the bloody one into an evidence bag. He didn't want any of his DNA on there. Then he filled the hole, covering it to make sure that no one could tell the ground had been disturbed.

As he drove back home, he passed the new Thorne construction site at the top of the hill. The view was astounding, rolling mountains that gave way to the clear blue lake. It had been a farm once, and now Thorne was turning it into a hotel.

A construction site was the perfect place to hide the glove. Thorne thought he was so clever, planting it to frame Sam. Now Kevin was going to turn the tables. He would sneak back late at night and bury it at the construction site, then at the right moment, when they were about to close in on Thorne, he'd tell Sam and Jo where to find it.

It was a good plan but risky. He'd have to time it perfectly. That glove could not be discovered until the very last minute, when they were about to lock Thorne away. Because Thorne would know who'd planted it, and once it came in as evidence, Kevin's life would be in danger unless Thorne wasn't in a position to order retaliation.

CHAPTER ELEVEN

S am wasn't surprised that no one was home at Scott Elliott's. Judging by the newspapers piled on the cement steps of the modest split-level ranch, it looked like no one had been there for almost a week. Since Dupont's murder.

"Nothing to see out back," Jo said as she trotted around from the back of the house, Lucy on her heels. "I looked in the windows. There's no sign of struggle."

Sam flipped up the top of the mailbox attached to the side of the house. Empty. "If Elliott hasn't been here, where's his mail?" Sam pointed to the pile of papers on the stoop. "The newspapers have piled up, but no mail."

Jo came to stand beside him and looked over his

shoulder into the mailbox. "You think someone took it?"

"No idea."

"You suppose he could've planned to go away, knowing he would be involved in Dupont's murder?"

"I don't think so. The meeting with Dupont wasn't planned. At least not that I know of. Dupont set the time and date, and that was only a few hours before we met." Sam turned to look at Jo. "How could Elliott have known in advance?"

"I remember last time I went on vacation, it took at least a week to stop the mail. I guess he really could be on vacation."

"You mean he might not even be involved. I suppose that's possible." Sam turned and looked over the suburban neighborhood. It had been developed about forty years ago, and the houses were spaced far apart with thick, mature landscaping between them.

It wasn't an upscale neighborhood. It was more the kind of neighborhood with elderly residents just hanging on to the homes they'd lived in all their lives. Maybe some of those neighbors were nosey. Sam made a mental note to canvass the neighborhood and ask the neighbors if they'd seen anything, even though he doubted they would have. With no signs of struggle and the fact that Jesse said that Scott never did business from home, he figured there would be little information to glean from the neighbors. Hell, Elliott really could just be on vacation.

Jo chewed her bottom lip as they walked down the steps together. "I don't know. This is all getting kind of weird. I'm nervous about Rita mentioning that SUV. I'm sure it was Mick's."

Sam nodded. He was sure it was Mick's too. "But Rita doesn't see very well, and she probably doesn't know what make or model she saw. How many SUVs do you think there are? Hopefully, she won't remember more about it." He took his phone from his pocket and texted Mick. "I'm giving Mick a heads-up. Plus, we need him to step up that investigation into the grandson. Now that we know that fingerprint links Tyler's and Dupont's cases, we need to continue to pursue that angle hard." He looked up at Jo. "I'm gonna meet him at Holy Spirits tonight. You in?"

"Definitely."

"Too bad Elliott's prints weren't in the database. He could be the killer, and he could know about Tyler's murder. We need to find him." Sam watched Lucy. She was honed in on a trash can, her nose working overtime.

"Maybe we could get a warrant and see if we can lift any fingerprints from inside the house," Jo suggested. "That would tell us if Elliott left the fingerprints."

"Might be hard to convince a judge that we have probable cause, but we can try." Sam headed to Lucy and lifted the lid on the trash barrel. The stench of sour milk and rotten vegetables stung his nose. He made a face and slammed the lid quickly. "Maybe we'll include the trash on the warrant. You never know what Scott Elliott might have thrown away. Lucy seems to have a keen nose."

"Right. I agree. Maybe Wyatt can look through the trash." Jo stepped back from the trash, her fingers pinching her nose.

"Yeah, and we don't want to have to keep lying to the sheriff." Sam slid a glance at her, and Jo grimaced. Sam had been surprised when she'd come up with the lie about the pigeons masking the noise of the SUV. He'd never known she was such a good liar. Made him wonder if she lied about anything else.

"I know. Sorry. I panicked. Tell the truth, even I was surprised that I could come up with a lie so quickly. It wasn't really a lie, though. I mean, those pigeons were loud, and anyway, it won't affect the outcome of the case because we know Mick didn't kill Dupont. In fact, my lie probably helped us. Having Mick as a suspect would only muddy the waters. It would take from resources looking for the actual killer." Jo glanced up at Sam from under her lashes, her gray eyes turning serious. "I wouldn't ever lie about anything big."

Something passed between them. Sam wasn't sure exactly what it was. Trust. Friendship. Something more? Sam nodded. "I know. I trust you. You did the right thing."

A look of relief spread across Jo's face, and Sam's gaze drifted to Lucy, now sitting by the truck. "Come on. We'd better get back to the station and get this warrant in process. I don't know if Judge Firth will grant it. We don't really have any evidence except Jessie telling us that Scott Elliott was his drug contact, and I'd kind of like to keep Jesse out of it. Plus, we don't want to tip our hand to Firth that we suspect Thorne in case he's in his pocket."

"It's worth a try. What else can we do?" Jo asked.

Sam opened the door to the truck and glanced back at the house. "I don't have a good feeling. If Elliott is involved, he would have information on Thorne. But where is Elliott? His disappearance is setting off alarm bells for me. He could be in danger. We need to bring him in alive so we can find out what he knows about Thorne."

CHAPTER TWELVE

J o went straight to her desk when they got back to the station. Sam had gone into his office with a stack of mail after instructing Reese on how to fill out the request for the warrant they needed to gain access to Scott Elliott's place. Jo didn't envy him the job of sorting through the mail. Judging by the way it was piling up on the corner of his desk, she knew that Sam didn't like the job any more than she did. He could have delegated it to one of them, but that was just like Sam to do the crap jobs himself instead of making someone else suffer.

A note from Wyatt sat on her desk. On it were the results of his research into the black SUV seen the night of Dupont's murder. Apparently, there were more than two thousand black SUVs registered in a thirty-mile radius. Good. That would make it nearly impossible to trace the vehicle to Mick.

Lucy had her nose in the trash can beside Jo's desk. She was sniffing hard enough to make the discarded doughnut bag crinkle. Jo leaned over and nudged the bag open.

"There's nothing in here but crumbs," she said to Lucy.

Lucy wagged her tail and cocked her head to the side.

"No, you eat enough treats. We don't want you to get fat."

The fur on Lucy's brow crinkled into a frown. She cast a longing glance at the bag then glared at Jo before trotting to her dog bed and pulling it into the pool of sunlight that streamed in from one of the large windows.

The dog really did have a good nose. Had Lucy smelled something important in the trash at Scott Elliott's, or had all that spoiled food drawn her interest? In previous cases, Lucy had proved that she'd had a nose for clues and not just food.

"What are you thinking?" Sam stood beside her desk, looking down at her.

"Just about Lucy sniffing the trash at Elliott's. Could be a clue in there."

"Or food. But anyway, Reese is putting the warrants together today. I'm going to have Kevin see if Scott Elliott was planning a trip."

Reese appeared in the squad room. "I've got that paperwork all set for the judge. Wyatt's out on a call, and Rita is coming in twenty minutes. Sheriff Hatch is on her way."

As if she'd been summoned by her words, they heard the lobby door open, and Bev Hatch came into the squad room. Reese went back to her desk after the two women exchanged greetings.

"Any luck with that contact?" Bev asked.

"Wasn't home. Looked like he'd been gone a while," Sam said.

Bev's left brow quirked up. "Left in a hurry?"

"Maybe."

"Interesting. Well, I have a couple of new things to report. The blood on the leaf matches Dupont's, so if we can match the fingerprint, we can tie that person to the crime scene."

"That will come in handy if we pull in some viable suspects," Sam said. "What's the other thing?"

"The lab found a small fragment of black hair in the chamber of the gun."

"A hair?" Sam asked, his eyes flicking to Jo. "Great!

Then we can get DNA from it. Narrow down the suspects by hair color."

Bev shook her head. "Not human. It was an animal hair."

Jo glanced at Lucy. Lucy hadn't been with them.

"Not sure the hair will help much. It was in the chamber, so it got in when the gun was loaded unless the chamber was opened after. There could have been animals in the mill, but I have no idea why the killer would open the chamber again. The presence of animals might explain some of the odd smudges the guys at the lab noticed when they blew up the photographs to do some mockups of the murder." Bev slid a suspicious side-eyed look at Sam and Jo. "Did you guys notice that?"

"We suspected the killer had moved stuff around the scene. So smudges didn't seem out of place," Sam said.

Bev nodded slowly, apparently satisfied with his explanation.

"I guess that makes sense."

The lobby door opened again, and Jo heard Reese greet Rita Hoelscher and direct her to the squad room. A few seconds later, Rita shuffled around the post office boxes, her hands full of miniature fruitcakes wrapped in colorful cellophane. Rita was a short, thin woman with a wild shock of white hair and wrinkles on her wrinkles. Her eyes flitted from Sam to Bev to Jo. Then she looked at the empty desks. "Where's that nice Officer Wyatt?"

"He's out at a fender bender," Sam said.

Rita's face collapsed in disappointment as Sam accepted the fruitcakes.

"But it's nice of you to come by, Rita," Sam said. "We'll see that he gets these."

Rita looked down at the fruitcakes. "Oh these are for all of you, not just Officer Wyatt."

Sam feigned excitement. "Oh, really? I get one too? That's awfully nice of you. Thank you so much."

Rita eyed them suspiciously, especially Bev. "Well, did you want something? Reese told me to come down."

Bev stepped forward, holding out her hand. "I'm Bev Hatch, the county sheriff. It's nice to meet you."

"Rita Hoelscher. Nice to meet you too." Her eyes slid to Sam. "Am I in trouble?"

Sam pulled out a chair and gestured for Rita to sit. "No, not at all, Rita. Wyatt told us that you saw a vehicle the night that Mayor Dupont was ... well, the other night."

Rita slowly crumpled into the chair. "I did. That's true."

"Could you tell us about it?" Bev asked.

Rita sat straighter. "Why, yes, I'd be happy to. I was walking Bitsy because she likes to walk in the woods. She loves to munch on those curly fiddlehead ferns." Rita stopped, slapping her hands to her cheeks and looking at Bev and Sam. "Oh dear, I hope those aren't endangered or anything. Is that why you called me in here?"

Sam smiled and patted Rita's hand. "No, not at all. We just want to hear about the vehicle."

"Oh, right. Well, we were walking along, and I heard the siren in the distance. It's always disturbing, you know." She glanced up at Sam and Bev. "So anyway, the walking trail that Bitsy likes is parallel to that old road that leads to the mill. I guess people use it as a shortcut, though I hardly ever see any cars except the UPS truck, the mailman, and of course, the garbageman."

Bev glanced at Jo and raised a brow. Sometimes it took witnesses a while to get to the point.

"I know the road," Sam said. "Now, do you remember what kind of vehicle it was? Did you see the driver?"

Rita scrunched up her face, causing her wrinkles to battle with each other for surface space. "No, I didn't see who was driving. The leaves were in the way, and it was going too fast. These young folks these days, they really need to slow down. Maybe you should put a speed trap up on that road," Rita suggested.

"We'll take that under advisement," Sam said.

Bev laid out photos of different SUVs on the desk in front of Rita. "Do you recognize what kind of SUV it was?" She pointed to a large photo of a Tahoe. "Was it a big one like this or a smaller one like this?" Bev's finger moved to a Kia Soul.

Rita put a forefinger to her lips. "I'm sorry. I'm not sure. They all look the same to me. I don't see how anyone can drive these big things. I can barely handle my Dodge Dart." Rita paused for a moment and looked thoughtful. "I do remember one thing, though. It had those big racks on the roof. You know, for luggage and stuff."

Bev nodded. "And you're sure you saw it when you heard the sirens."

"Yes, ma'am. The sirens were loud, and Bitsy doesn't like loud noises or fast cars. She was spooked, so we had to turn around and go right home."

"Did you see where it came from or which way it went?" Bev asked.

Rita looked at Sam as if Bev had just asked the stupidest question. "Only one place it could come from: that old mill. Reed's Ferry. And only one place it could go to: Foster Street."

Sam looked at Bev. "Foster Street leads out to the main road. Could've been headed anywhere."

Sam turned his attention back to Rita, crouching down to talk to her at eye level. "Okay, Rita, you did good. Now I want you to go home and think about this and let us know if you remember anything more."

"Okay." Rita got up. "I can go now?"

"Yep. You have a nice day."

"Nice to meet you," Bev said.

"You too. Enjoy the fruitcake."

Rita shuffled off, and Bev turned back to Sam and Jo.

"Well, that wasn't much help. There have to be thousands of black SUVs around." Bev picked up the photos of the SUVs and sighed.

Jo held up the note from Wyatt. "Two-thousand-three-hundred and forty-one, to be exact. At least that's how many have been registered in a thirty-mile radius, according to Wyatt's research."

"Let's not forget the SUV might not be one registered around here," Sam said.

"Yeah, it's not much of a lead," Bev said.

"So we're not much more ahead of where we were yesterday," Sam said.

"What about the hair?" Jo asked. "Can we get anything off of that?"

Bev shook her head. "There's not much to go on with that. We already know the killer moved stuff around. Until we have some suspects, the hair is meaningless. Looks like our best hope is to locate this Scott Elliott."

The lobby door opened, and Harry rushed in. "Hey, I ran into Rita Hoelscher, and she said she left some fruitcake ..." His eyes fell on the packages on the desk. "Oh, there it is. Do you mind if I cut myself a piece? I do love her fruitcake, and she doesn't bake it often."

Bev, Jo, and Sam exchanged a glance.

"Not at all," Bev said.

"Take as much as you want," Sam added.

"You can have all of mine." Jo gestured toward one of the loaves.

Bev nodded. "Mine too. In fact, take it all with you."

"You sure? I wouldn't want to deprive you ..." Harry glanced from Bev to Sam to Jo, who all nodded enthusiastically.

"Please help yourself."

Harry's eyes lit up, and he grabbed one of the packages and opened it. He turned to Bev as he popped a piece in his mouth. "Hey, kid, what brings you down here again?"

"Helping out with the Dupont case."

Harry's eyes narrowed as he nibbled the fruitcake. Lucy came to sit beside him, turning pleading eyes up to him. "Oh, nasty business, that."

"Indeed."

"Though I think we can do better for mayor." Harry tossed a little piece of fruitcake to Lucy then bent down to her level. Lucy put her paw up, and Harry shook it before giving her another piece, standing, and brushing crumbs from his tan chinos. "Well, I better get going. The missus will be looking for me. Thanks for the fruitcake."

"I'll walk you out. It's almost quitting time," Bev said. "How is Mabel, anyway?"

"Fine, fine. Getting ready to go to Florida already. See you later, Sam."

Bev turned and gave them a two-finger wave. "Let me know if you locate that lead."

Jo looked out the window as they disappeared around the edge of the post office boxes. The sun was low in the sky, casting long shadows from the oak trees in the town common.

"Quitting sounds good," Sam said. "You ready to

head to Holy Spirits? Reese is working late; she can stay with Lucy."

"I sure am. And I could really use a drink."

***

"I DON'T THINK we have to worry about Mick's SUV being identified at the mill," Sam said to Jo when they were seated at the bar in Holy Spirits.

"Hopefully not." Jo took a pull on her beer. She seemed a bit down, and Sam wondered if the case was getting to her. Heck, it was getting to him.

"Rita won't remember, and no one else has come forward, so we can put that worry behind us." Sam glanced up at the mirror behind the bar, where he saw the simple round tables and maple chairs behind him. Patches of red, blue, and green spilled in from the stained-glass windows above the mirror. Toward the door, two of the original long oak pews sat near the door, a table between them. Sam liked to watch the surprised looks on tourists' faces as they entered. Many of them mistook the bar for an actual church because the vestibule looked exactly as it had when Holy Spirits was a church. It wasn't until you opened those big oak double doors that you realized that instead of an altar with a cross and candles, there was a bar with liquor bottles and bar stools.

It didn't take long to figure out there wasn't any preaching going on in here unless your idea of preaching included yelling at whatever sports team on the television was losing.

Sam turned his attention back to his beer on the polished wood of the bar and let the din of conversation behind him fade as he took a swig. The smell of burgers and fries permeated the room, reminding his stomach that it was suppertime.

"What do you think of the hair?" Jo asked.

"Grasping at straws." Sam spied the owner of Holy Spirits, Billie Hanson, at the end of the bar. Her lavender-tinged spiked hair bobbed up and down as she juggled pulling a beer with serving a burger. He caught her eye and tapped his bottle to indicate he was ready for another.

"That's what I thought too, but still, maybe Scott Elliott has a pet or ... I don't know." Jo swung her bar stool around to face away from the bar. Sam could see the wheels in her head turning as she tried to figure out how they could use the hair. Could they? Bev had said it was in the chamber, which indicated the hair was in there when the killer loaded the gun. But how would an animal hair help them? It certainly wasn't going to help them *find* the killer, but maybe once they did, it could help them prove he'd done it.

Or had the hair been planted? If someone was trying to frame him, it wouldn't be hard to get one of Lucy's hairs and plant it in the gun.

"Here comes Mick." Jo inclined her head toward the door.

Sam glanced in the mirror to see his best friend walk into the bar. Mick was tall and broad. The black T-shirt stretched across his chest made it obvious that he still spent a lot of time working out, even though he was pushing forty. Apparently, it was too hot for his usual black leather jacket. His light-blue eyes scanned the bar, falling on Sam and Jo. He took the stool next to Sam, leaning across him to greet Jo.

Billie slid Sam's beer across the bar and looked at Mick. "Usual?"

Mick nodded.

Billie pulled out a tumbler, threw in some ice, and splashed it full of whiskey before setting it in front of Mick.

Mick took a swig, let out a breath, and turned to Sam and Jo. "So what's up? Fill me in."

They ordered a basket of sweet potato fries and shared it as they brought Mick up to speed. Sam and Jo took turns telling him how Rita had seen his SUV, how

Jamison had pulled Bev Hatch onto the case, how Jesse had given them the name of his supplier, and how the fingerprint was tied to both Tyler's and Dupont's murder scenes.

"So you don't think Rita will be able to identify my vehicle?" Mick asked.

"Nah." Sam swigged his beer.

"Good. Damn, that's interesting about the fingerprint. I know that old lady's grandson has something to do with the stolen car." Mick swirled his glass, the ice cubes clinking. He swigged the rest of it down and chomped on a cube. "Makes me nervous with Bev Hatch on the case, though."

"Yeah, she's pretty sharp," Jo said.

"And honest," Sam said.

"We're honest, too," Jo said.

Mick raised a brow. "Yeah, but in a roundabout way. Doesn't Bev know your dad or something, Sam?"

"My grandpa helped her mom out a bit, but I doubt that'll hold much weight if she thinks we've done something wrong."

"You don't expect me to believe that she's never done anything wrong?" Mick nodded for a refill as Billie swooped by with the whiskey bottle. "Anyone who has been in law enforcement for a while has done something that ain't quite on the up-and-up. Don't expect me to believe she never pushed the envelope, never had to do something a little bit outside of the law to make sure a killer didn't go free."

"I don't know if she did or not," Sam said.

"Count on it. Any sheriff worth his or her salt is forced to, but that's beside the point. We'll just make sure she doesn't catch wind of anything you guys might have done wrong." Mick raised his brows and took a gulp of his drink.

"I don't know about that, but I know one thing: the sooner we get rid of Thorne, the better. For all of us."

"You can say that again." Mick's expression turned somber, and Sam thought about the knife. Thorne still had it, so Mick had as much at stake as anyone to get rid of him.

"Sounds like things hinge on that fingerprint, and the only lead we have on that is the grandson and possibly this Scott Elliott," Sam said. "We need to talk to these people alone first. One of them might know where Tyler kept that box. There's no telling what's in there. We might not want anyone else to get a look at it."

"Right. So you guys work on Elliott, and I'll work on the grandson." Mick took another sip of his whiskey, his face thoughtful. "Something doesn't add up, though."

"Lots of things don't add up," Jo said.

Mick swung his stool to face them and put his elbow on the bar, leaning in closer to Sam and Jo. "You said that the fingerprint found in the car when Tyler was killed matched the one on the leaf near the mill. The same person was at both places."

"Yeah, but we don't know who that is. The fingerprint didn't match anyone in the database."

"Right. But we do know that *Tyler* knew that person. And if that person was at the roadside when Tyler was killed, he is probably tight with Thorne. If that's the case, then that person likely broke some laws somewhere along the way."

Realization dawned on Sam. That was what he loved about Mick. He could always count on him to come up with a logical solution. "And if he did break some laws, Tyler might have covered for him."

Mick smiled and nodded.

"But where does this Scott Elliott fit in? He's never been fingerprinted."

"Could be the person who was with Tyler was higher up. Elliott is low on the pole, right?"

"Yep," Sam agreed. "We're trying for a warrant to lift a print from his house."

"This could be another lead," Jo said. "We can look

through Tyler's calls to see if there was anyone he might have let off the hook."

Sam glanced at her. "That's a great idea. See? This case is starting to open up."

Jo tilted her beer bottle and clinked it with Mick's and Sam's. "Great. I'll get on that first thing in the morning."

CHAPTER THIRTEEN

J o got in early the next day. She wanted to research Tyler's arrest records without everyone else in the office figuring out what she was doing. Too bad everyone else had the same idea about coming in early.

Sam was already in his office with Lucy, the door slightly ajar. Reese was at the reception desk, handing out permits for yard sales. Kevin was typing a report. Jo noticed he seemed a little jittery, glancing up as if she'd caught him at something whenever she walked past his desk. She guessed the case was getting to everyone. Especially her. But that might be good, because it was taking up all her thinking time, and for the first time in years, she hadn't thought about her sister's case. That was a good sign, a sign that it really was time to put her sister's case behind her.

She didn't want anyone to know what she was doing, so she sat at her desk, typing on her laptop. The squad room was quiet, the sound of laptop keys clacking and the smell of coffee permeating the air. At the front desk, Reese was trying to referee an argument between Joan Cummings and Myrtle Winters. Both Joan and Myrtle wanted to have yard sales at the weekend, but they each felt the other's sale would take traffic away from their sale and were trying to convince Reese to deny the permit to the other.

Jo let the squabble become background noise and focused on her work. Tyler had gone on a lot of calls this past year, and some of them were a little odd.

"Is there anything I can help you with?" Wyatt's question startled her. He leaned over to look at her screen.

Jo closed her laptop. "No, thanks."

Wyatt gave her a funny look and then turned to go back to his desk. "Okay. Let me know if you do. I finished up my paperwork."

As Wyatt walked back to his desk, Kevin spun around in his chair and handed him some papers. "Here. You can type these up if you're looking for something to do."

Wyatt took them silently and got to work.

Jo reopened her computer, her pulse quickening when she noticed a few discrepancies. There was one person Tyler had noted in a few calls, but he never brought that person in. Forest Duncan. It could be a coincidence. She needed to dig deeper to see if there was any pattern.

"Holy crap!" Reese's excited voice carried over the post office boxes, and Jo glanced up. Apparently, the yard sale arguers were gone, because the only sound that came from over the wall of post office boxes was the rustling of papers. Lucy must have heard, too, because she trotted out, followed closely by Sam. Reese appeared around the post office boxes, a piece of paper in her hand.

"What is it?" Kevin asked.

"I got an ID on that fingerprint. The one from the crime scene. I had a flag in the system for them to fax it to me if anyone got a hit. And someone got a hit."

"Really?" Wyatt stood up at his desk. "That's great. We got a break in the case."

"Yeah, part of it's great," Reese said. "The print did belong to that guy you were looking for yesterday—Scott Elliott."

Jo's spirits picked up. "I knew he was involved."

Apparently, all that work Sam had done to groom Jesse had paid off.

"Let's go pick him up." Sam pulled his keys from his pocket. "Where did the hit come from? I assume he was arrested and printed."

"Figured it was only a matter of time before he'd be arrested." Jo jumped up from her chair to join Sam.

"Yeah, that's the part that isn't so great," Reese said, stopping Jo in her tracks. "You can't pick him up."

"Why not?"

"He's dead."

Sam pressed his lips together and glanced at Jo. They needed Elliott alive to find the person further up the chain. Jo glanced back at her laptop. Unless ... This Forest Duncan guy might be closer to the top. If he had been involved with Tyler and Tyler was Thorne's son, Tyler must have been pretty close to the top, and it made sense the top minions would work together.

Maybe if they pulled Forest in, they'd get all the information they needed. Maybe it didn't matter that Elliott was dead. But Jo couldn't mention that in front of anyone else. If she did, she'd have to explain why they were looking into Tyler, and then they'd have to explain about the DNA paper they'd taken off of Dupont's body. Bringing up the fact that she was looking into a pattern on whom Tyler had arrested and released would mean that they'd have to admit they'd been holding back evidence on his case.

"Dead? How?" Kevin asked.

The lobby door opened, and Bev Hatch came around the post office boxes with a white doughnut bag from Brewed Awakening in her hand. She took one look at their faces and said, "I see you've heard the news."

Sam turned to her. "You mean that the print from the leaf got a hit but the suspect is dead?"

Bev nodded once. "Yeah, found in a shallow grave down in Belknap County."

"Murdered. So he killed Dupont, and then someone killed him to cover it up." Sam brushed his hands through his short hair. "We just lost our best lead."

"He might not be the killer." Bev passed Sam the bag.

"What?" Sam passed the bag along to Jo without taking a doughnut.

"It's still early, and I didn't get the full report, but I talked to Dean Adams, the medical examiner handling the autopsy. He said there was no gunpowder residue on Elliott's hands."

"Well, it's been more than a week since Dupont

was killed. I'm sure it would be gone by now," Sam said.

"No. Elliott's been dead for a week at least, he thinks. If he died right after the murder and he pulled the trigger, he'd likely still have residue. Look, we already knew more than one person was at the scene where Dupont was murdered. This Elliott guy was probably killed because he witnessed it. Maybe he wasn't even working with the killer. Maybe he just stumbled on it." Bev shrugged. "I have no idea. But we'll work closely with the investigation into his death. Maybe we can get some leads."

"Let's hope so," Sam said.

"I'm in touch with the sheriff in Belknap County, but now that we have a solid link between Tyler and Dupont, I think we need to start going over Tyler's case again." Bev looked at Sam out of the corner of her eye, and Jo's heart clenched as she picked out a jelly doughnut and passed the bag to Kevin. The narrow-eyed look told her that Bev suspected something might not be on the up-and-up.

"Sure," Sam said. "But we need to find out more about Elliott and his death and —"

Bev held up a hand. "Yes. I'm on that. But I'm going to use Kevin and Wyatt while you, Jo, and I go over Tyler's case."

Sam frowned, but Jo figured he knew better than to argue with Bev; arguing might make her suspicious. "Okay."

Jo sat at her desk, her gaze flicking from Sam to Bev, watching the conversation and trying not to open her big mouth lest she say something incriminating.

Bev looked at Kevin. "Kevin, you go to the medical examiner's office and wait for that autopsy report. Hurry him along. He's supposed to fax it here, but I know he works faster when someone's there, putting the pressure on." She turned to Wyatt and handed him a yellow sticky note. "Wyatt, you go down and talk to Bobby Sampson. He's in charge of the scene where they found the body. Tell him that you want all the photos of the crime scene. Maybe we can see something that jogs a memory that links it to the Dupont killing."

Kevin and Wyatt cast questioning glances at Sam.

Sam nodded, and they left.

"I guess we don't need that search warrant after all," Sam said.

"That's good 'cause it got rejected," Reese said before turning to go back to the lobby. "I'll be at my desk if you guys need me to look anything up."

"Okay. I want to look at everything you have from Tyler's case," Bev said.

"The state police took over the case early on, so we don't have much," Sam said.

"Don't give me that crap. Any good cop would investigate a fallen officer's death on the side. And I think you're a good cop, Sam. I'm trusting you because your grandpa was a good man and helped my mom out, so I kind of owe you one." Bev crossed her arms over her chest and looked at Sam hard for a few seconds before adding, "Don't make me regret it."

"WHAT DO you think that was all about?" Wyatt asked as he and Kevin jogged down the front steps of the police station.

Kevin glanced over at him. The question had a suspicious undertone that Kevin didn't like. In fact, Kevin was starting to not like Wyatt at all. There was something predatory about him, as though he were watching and waiting for something to go down so he could pounce. What that was, Kevin had no idea.

Maybe it was Kevin's own guilt that was making him suspicious. He really had no right to suspect Wyatt. The guy hadn't done anything wrong, at least not that Kevin knew about.

Kevin shrugged, acting casual. "You know how the

higher-ups are. They probably wanted to strategize or something. Let us do the grunt work."

Wyatt glanced back at the station. "Huh. Seems kind of like important grunt work. But I'm happy to be doing it."

Kevin stopped at the Crown Vic, and Wyatt hesitated then looked toward the small parking lot beside the building.

"I'll take my car. It's good on gas," Wyatt offered.

Kevin opened the door of the Crown Vic. Damn straight he'd take his personal vehicle. Kevin didn't like that Wyatt was insinuating that maybe it would be his place to take the Crown Vic. Kevin had been there longer; he should drive it. But Kevin didn't want to say any of that out loud. There was no sense starting something with the guy. And ultimately, it was up to Sam who drove the car, so he simply said, "Okay. See you later."

Kevin watched Wyatt trot off and then slid into the car, the soft seats and smell of sunbaked leather surrounding him as he started the engine.

He really should give Wyatt a break. As near as he could tell, Wyatt was only trying to be helpful. The weird vibe he picked up was probably just because Wyatt was new and trying to fit in. Kevin was out of sorts with of all the strange things about this case—and his own secrets were grating on him.

Kevin had a bad feeling about what Bev Hatch might find when they looked into Tyler's case. He'd suspected Tyler was up to something before he was even killed. Of course, back then, he'd thought Tyler was doing something against the law, that his contact worked in law enforcement and was trying to get evidence on him.

Now Kevin wasn't so sure. He was sure that his contact worked for Thorne. His contact had wanted Kevin to search Tyler's belongings for electronic data, so it stood to reason that Tyler was one of the good guys. He was working against Thorne. Or was he working with him, and Thorne wanted to make sure he didn't turn on him? Maybe Thorne had been looking for leverage.

Kevin's thoughts turned to the thumb drive tucked away in his kitchen. If Bev found something that got Sam and Jo into trouble, Kevin would hand the drive over to Sam. There could be something on it that got Sam and Jo out of trouble—or there could be something that got them in deeper. Either way, Sam could do what he wanted with it. But he would only turn the drive over if it was necessary. He didn't want Sam to know he'd betrayed them by taking the drive in the first place.

He waved to Wyatt as he drove past, the funny feeling coming over him again. Earlier that morning, before anyone else had come in, Wyatt had mentioned that he'd seen Sam talking to a guy standing next to a black SUV with a roof rack similar to the vehicle Rita had said she'd seen driving away from the mill. By the description of the man and the fact that Wyatt had seen them outside Holy Spirits, Kevin figured it was Mick Gervasi, Sam's best friend. Kevin seemed to recall that Mick drove a black SUV.

Had Mick been at Reed's Ferry Mill the night Dupont was killed? It was possible. Kevin knew that Sam used Mick for some of his investigations. But what did it matter? If Mick was there, Kevin figured Sam had good reason.

He'd brushed off Wyatt's question by pointing out there were thousands of black SUVs. Maybe he could do something more to deflect suspicion. He'd have to think on that. What if the SUV really belonged to someone else and it was a good lead? He wouldn't want to try to cover that up. But no, he was sure that it was Mick, because if Sam didn't already know who it was, he would have jumped on the lead a little harder.

Kevin knew that Sam and Jo kept some secrets about that crime scene. The lawn-mowing neighbor had said Jo had been there earlier in the afternoon, but Sam and Jo never put that in the report. Sure, it was a minor thing and even understandable that Jo might come to scout things out earlier, but the fact that they never mentioned it made Kevin think there might be more going on.

Kevin didn't care. Guilt over what he'd previously done made him more determined to make sure that Sam and Jo came out on the clean end of this and that Thorne went away for good. And not only because his own life was in jeopardy if he continued to feed fake information to his contact, but because it was the right thing to do.

Kevin drove off, his plan firmly in place. He'd keep an eye on Wyatt. And he still had his ace in the hole—the glove. He just hoped that by using it, he wouldn't be signing his own death warrant.

CHAPTER FOURTEEN

S am walked Bev through everything they had on
Tyler's case. Well, at least, everything he wanted
her to know. He didn't want to let on too much of what
they'd been investigating on the side, and he certainly
wasn't going to tell her about the DNA test or the
mysterious key.

The whole time they reviewed the case with Bev,
Jo had acted odd. She was quieter than usual, tapping
her pencil on her notepad faster than usual. She'd
scarfed down two of the jelly doughnuts that Bev had
brought, and Sam got the impression she was bursting
to tell him something.

"So that's it?" Bev asked. "Not much to go on."

"We didn't have much time to investigate," Sam

said. "With Tyler gone, we were short-handed, and another murder happened right away. Actually, there have been a couple of murders to investigate, so ..." Sam shrugged and let his sentence trail off.

"And you found his log in his car, denoting that he was stopping to help a car in distress?" Bev pointed to the log, and Sam's heart hitched. Would she notice the difference in writing Jo had entered for Tyler?

"Yeah. Looks like that last entry was made quickly." Sam paused and tilted his head to look at the log. "I don't know if maybe he suspected something at that stop, and that's why he scribbled in just the bare minimum."

"But he never called in anything suspicious," Bev said.

"We don't have a dispatcher that time of night. He could have called me if he needed backup."

Bev nodded. "Guess he didn't think he needed it."

Sam rubbed his chin. "Truth is, I feel responsible for what happened to Tyler. It happened under my watch. Maybe I should have been the one out there that night."

"Nah. You can't feel that way, Sam," Bev said. "It's part of the job. It's what we sign on for. Tyler knew that."

Bev's phone dinged. She pulled it from her back pocket and looked at the display. "Okay. Gotta run. I'll let you know if anything else comes up. We'll meet back here in a few hours to see what Kevin and Wyatt found out."

"Okay," Sam said.

Sam waited for the lobby door to close and then turned to Jo. "Okay, what is it? I know you've been dying to tell me something."

"Yeah, I wasn't sure if I should say it in front of Bev, but I think I have a good lead." Jo rushed to her desk and opened her computer. "I've been going over Tyler's arrest, and I think I'm on to something here."

She turned the display toward Sam, and he bent closer.

"Check out this guy. Forest Duncan. It looks like Tyler went on a few calls associated with his name, but he never brought him in."

Sam was dubious. "That doesn't necessarily mean anything. But I guess it's *something*. What kind of calls? Was he the one calling in or the one being called *on*?"

"He was the one doing something wrong. Minor stuff, though, so stands to reason he wouldn't be arrested. But wait until you see this." Jo turned the computer back toward her, typed something in, and then angled the display back toward Sam. "Guess what Forest Duncan does for a living."

Sam leaned closer. Duncan worked for the sanitation department. He was the garbageman.

"The garbageman," Sam said. "I thought the name looked familiar. That would give him an excuse to drive all around town and stop at houses, just as Jesse said."

"Remember how Lucy was sniffing the garbage cans at Scott Elliott's house? Maybe she smelled something from the crime scene or a connection between Elliott and Duncan." Jo leaned back in her chair. "But I suppose we can't tell Bev that we're talking to a lead based on Lucy smelling garbage."

"Maybe not, but Bev actually gave us the perfect reason to find this lead."

"She did?"

Sam nodded. "By her request to look deeper into Tyler's case, we now have a reason to research the calls he went on. And as such, we noticed the name Forest Duncan came up a few times and remembered he was a municipal employee."

"Combined with what Jesse told us about Thorne's distributor being a government employee whose job allowed him to be all around town and at various houses, I'd say that's a good reason to question him."

Sam pulled the keys to the Tahoe from his pocket. "Exactly. And I can't think of a better time to do that than right now."

CHAPTER FIFTEEN

F orest Duncan lived in a duplex clad in dirt-smudged aluminum siding on the outskirts of town. It was late afternoon when Jo and Sam arrived. Sam knew the garbage was collected early in the morning, so he figured Forest would be home. The rusted-out red Hyundai in the driveway told him he'd figured right.

Jo looked at the house skeptically. "This doesn't look like the type of place one of Thorne's distributors would live in. Wouldn't they be able to afford something better than this?"

"Maybe it's a front. It would seem pretty suspicious if the town garbageman lived in a mansion."

"Good point. He might spend his money on expensive toys and interior upgrades." Jo got out of the passenger side and let Lucy out of the back, and they all walked to the front door.

A short, pudgy guy in his midthirties with large, round black-framed glasses that magnified his blue eyes to comical proportions answered the knock. His eyes widened nervously when they fell on Lucy and enlarged even further when Sam and Jo showed their badges.

"Can I help you?" He cracked the door only a few inches. Sam wondered if he'd refuse to talk to them and slam the door in their faces.

"We just have a few questions," Sam said.

"About what?"

Sam craned his neck to look inside. The living room was furnished with yard sale furniture in vintage 1970s plaid. A cheap particleboard coffee table covered in dings and with chipped corners sat in front of the couch. There was a decent-sized TV on the wall. If Forest Duncan had a lot of money, he sure wasn't spending it on his décor. Maybe he was socking it away for retirement. Sam made a mental note to check into his finances.

"The mayor's murder," Jo piped in. Sam noticed her eyes trained on Forest. She was studying his reaction to her words. That was what Jo did best. She had a degree in criminal psychology and was always looking for some sort of tell or sign people were lying. She was good at that sort of thing. Sam, not so much. He was better at putting together the physical evidence. But together, they made a pretty tight team.

Forest backed up a step, pulling the door tighter. "I don't know anything about a murder."

"You're not a suspect. We just think you might have seen something because of your job with the sanitation department." Sam's assurance seemed to work. Duncan's shoulders relaxed, and he opened the door wider.

"Can we come in?" Sam asked.

Duncan thought for a few seconds and then nodded, glancing at Lucy. "The dog too? I don't much like dogs."

"She's harmless," Jo said. As if to reassure him, Lucy cocked her head to the side and gave a friendly whine.

"Okay. I guess so." Duncan opened the door wider, and they entered.

Duncan shuffled backward to give Lucy a wide berth as the three of them spilled into the living room. The place was small. A gold-shag-carpeted living room opened to a kitchen, where dirty dishes mounded in the sink. It smelled like macaroni and cheese and hot dogs.

Lucy must have approved of the odor, considering the way her nose twitched high in the air. Sam scanned the dishes on the counter, and something caught his eye. A navy-blue coffee mug with large white letters. From the way the mug was turned, he could only make out two of the letters, a *W* and an *R*.

"I think you knew Officer Richardson, didn't you?" Sam asked.

Forest blinked his owlish eyes and looked down at the floor. "Richardson? Maybe. I know a few officers because of my job. Was he the one who got killed?"

"Yes." Sam glanced at Jo, who raised her left brow a barely noticeable amount.

"Sorry about that." Forest looked back up at him. "So is that what you came to ask?"

"No. I just thought you were friends, for some reason."

Forest shrugged and stared blankly at Sam.

"So, back to the business at hand. Were you working the day of the mayor's murder?" Sam asked.

"Yeah. I work every day except Monday and Tuesday," Duncan answered Sam, but his eyes were fixed on Lucy, who sniffed around the coffee table.

"Your route takes you past Reed's Ferry Mill, right?" Jo asked.

"Well, I don't actually go to the mill. There's no

one living there, so no garbage." Forest was distracted by Lucy, who had trotted into the kitchen and was sniffing in the direction of the counter. "What is she doing?"

"Nothing." Jo snapped her fingers. "Lucy, heel!"

Lucy obediently came to Jo's side, and Forest focused his attention back on Sam.

"But your truck was seen on the dirt road near the mill that day," Sam said. He wasn't actually sure if the truck was seen there *that* day. Rita had only said she saw it there sometimes. But he figured it might rile Forest up a bit to tell him that someone had seen him at the murder scene.

But Forest didn't seem riled. He seemed thoughtful. "Okay, I do cut through there. Otherwise, I'd have to go all the way back out Bartlett Street and then onto Cherryvale and then to Forester. I'd have to backtrack the streets I'd already been on. I figure I'm saving the town gas money to cut through that road."

"We do appreciate that," Sam said.

"Besides, the day the mayor was killed, my route was on the other side of town. I do different sections each day so that everyone gets pickup once a week. And wasn't he killed at night, anyway?"

"Yep, 'round suppertime," Sam said.

"Well, then I wouldn't have seen anything because

my route ends at two p.m. So by suppertime, I'm at home, playing video games." Forest gestured toward the TV, where Sam saw a video game in pause mode. "So I wouldn't have been anywhere near the mill when the mayor was killed."

Sam exchanged a glance with Jo. He couldn't sense if Forest was lying or not. The guy seemed the type to get nervous if he was guilty, but if he was one of Thorne's distributors, he might be good at acting.

What Forest had told them made sense, though. Sam was going to have to do his due diligence and check it out. In the meantime, they had no reason to pull him in. "Okay, well, thank you. If you do think of anything or hear anything, would you please let us know?"

Forest nodded. "Of course."

Jo and Sam said goodbye and headed back to the Tahoe.

"So what do you think about that?" Sam asked as he pulled out of the driveway.

"He seemed nervous at first and when you asked about Tyler, but when I asked about Dupont's murder, he didn't appear unduly shocked. I didn't see any of the usual tells," Jo said. "But he could be an accomplished liar. I think we need to keep investigating."

"Me too. I have a funny feeling that Forest

Duncan is involved. I'm pretty sure he was lying. And he knew Tyler better than he lets on," Sam said.

Jo glanced over. "Why's that?"

"He had a White Rock Police Department mug on his counter. Now where do you think he got that if he wasn't in cahoots with someone in the department?"

CHAPTER SIXTEEN

Wyatt, Kevin, and Bev were back in the squad room by the time Jo and Sam returned to the station. Wyatt had gotten the crime scene photos as Bev had requested, and they'd tacked them on the corkboard.

The photos were about what Sam had expected. A dirty shallow grave covered with leaves. A pale body with a gunshot wound in the head. Sam's stomach churned. He'd seen worse, but it never ceased to amaze him to see the violence people could inflict on one another.

Lucy trotted over and sat down next to Bev, staring up at the photos as if going over the case along with them.

Bev turned. "Glad you guys are back. We got the

crime scene photos, and we're going over what the investigating detective told me."

"Anything new?" Sam asked.

"Afraid not." Bev consulted the notes on her cell phone as she paced around the squad room, spewing information. "Victim was buried in a shallow grave, single gunshot to the head.45-caliber bullet. No gun found. So far, no idea who did it."

"According to the medical examiner down there, Elliott can't be the killer," Kevin said. "Turns out Scott Elliott was killed not long after Dupont, and he had no gunpowder residue on his hands."

"So maybe that fingerprint on the leaf was Elliott running away from Dupont's killer?" Jo asked.

"Who knows? Do you think he was just an innocent witness?" Sam asked. "Jesse said he was a cog in Thorne's drug dealing, so I doubt he was very innocent."

"True, but it's a big leap from being a small-time drug dealer to a murderer," Jo pointed out. "He might have become frightened and bolted."

Bev pursed her lips. "If so, how do you explain his fingerprint at the crime scene of Officer Richardson's death? Seems he'd be used to murder after being involved in a cop killing."

"Elliott might not have been in the car when

Richardson was killed. The fingerprint could have been left earlier," Wyatt said.

Bev turned toward Wyatt. "Good point. But let's say he was with Dupont's killer. Why would he have been outside the mill?"

"Making sure they didn't leave any evidence?" Wyatt suggested.

"Why would they worry about that? They wouldn't have been near the spot where Kevin found the leaf." Sam turned to Kevin. "You said you found it behind the mill?"

"Yep. Near the walking path."

"The killer would have parked in front. That's where the parking lot is."

"Might have parked on side roads so the vehicles wouldn't be seen," Kevin offered. "The neighbors around there keep a close eye on comings and goings."

"It's all a mystery, and that's what we need to dig into." Bev looked thoughtful as she continued to pace, her eyes on the floor. "My question is, what is the tie-in with this Elliott guy and Officer Richardson? Do you think Richardson was investigating Elliott?"

"If he was, I didn't know about it. Seems to me, though, that Elliott is connected with Thorne." Sam pointed to the photo of the shallow grave. "This looks like Thorne's work. We already know Elliott was at the mill, and it's no coincidence he ended up dead hours later."

"Maybe he freaked out and they were afraid he would get a case of nerves and tell the cops," Jo said.

"I still have a feeling this whole thing is somehow tied into Tyler Richardson's murder. And there's no physical evidence that leads to Thorne." Bev glanced at Sam. "Not that I don't think the guy is capable, but you have to bring me more to go on. Meanwhile, don't let your vendetta against him color the way you see the case."

Was that what he was doing? Misinterpreting the clues? But that piece of paper in Dupont's hand, linking Tyler and Thorne, was physical proof. Too bad he couldn't tell anyone about it. Not to mention the reason for meeting with Dupont in the mill in the first place. "Don't forget that Dupont was going to give us information that could nail Thorne. Who would have a better motive? That's the main reason Thorne is number one on my list."

Bev pressed her lips together, still pacing. "Point taken. I checked ballistics. Richardson, Elliott, and Dupont weren't killed with the same gun."

"They never did find the gun that killed Tyler," Kevin said.

"Yeah, well, criminals have a way of making guns disappear," Jo said.

"Or rendering them untraceable, like the one that killed Dupont," Bev added.

"You might be on to something with your idea that Tyler was investigating on his own," Sam said. "After we went over Tyler's case with you, we decided to dig a little further into his calls. I might have a viable suspect."

Bev turned from her pacing, her brows notched up. "Really?"

Sam told Bev, Kevin, and Wyatt how they'd stumbled across Forest Duncan's name and about their visit to his home. Sam played up the idea that Tyler was investigating Forest in connection with Thorne, maybe even grooming him as an informant as Sam had done with Jesse. It wasn't so much that he was protecting Tyler, but he couldn't give away what he knew about Tyler's connection to Thorne without making himself and Jo look bad.

"That does sound promising," Bev said. "But now we need to find something to tie him to this case. Did he have any pets?"

"I didn't see any," Jo said. "He was afraid of Lucy, though, so I'm pretty sure he doesn't have a dog."

"You're thinking about the hair found in the gun?" Sam looked at Bev.

Bev nodded.

"Forest didn't seem keen on dogs, but maybe the hair isn't from a dog," Sam said. "Do you know what species of animal it was from?"

"I can find out." Bev continued talking as she typed a text on her phone. "So what priors does this Forest Duncan have?"

"Uh, well, none. We just noticed he was mentioned in some of the police calls Tyler went out on."

Bev looked up from her phone, her brows knitting. "But he was never arrested?"

"Nope."

Bev's frown deepened. "If he's a drug dealer, you'd think he would have been in trouble or arrested."

"You'd think," Sam said.

"And Officer Richardson never brought him in, even though he was implicated in these calls. What were they?" Bev's voice was tinged with skepticism, and that made Sam's gut tighten. He could tell she was growing suspicious of Tyler. She wouldn't be a good cop if she weren't feeling some of the same suspicions he was.

"Mostly minor stuff. Disturbing the peace. One

count of lurking. If he was grooming him, he'd have let him off." *Or if he was protecting him.*

"Okay, well, this Forest Duncan is definitely a person of interest," Bev said.

"I'm gonna look into his finances. His house was a dump, but I figure if he's running drugs for Thorne, he's gotta have a stash somewhere. Maybe he's investing it or something." Sam shrugged. "His bank account might give us something to go on. You know how it is. We have to build the case one clue at a time."

"And Elliott's trash wasn't picked up," Jo said. "I'm gonna check what day he has pickup. It just might be another thing we can use to prove that Forest Duncan had ties to Scott Elliott."

"How so?" Wyatt asked.

"Well, if Forest already knew that Scott Elliott was dead, why would he pick up the trash?"

"Huh. Okay, that's stretching it a little, but everything we can look into counts," Bev said.

"What about an alibi?" Bev asked.

"He says he was at home, playing video games, when Dupont died."

The lobby door opened, and they fell silent. Sam figured it was probably one of the locals, wanting a yard sale permit or to pay the water bill. He didn't want whoever it was to overhear gruesome murder talk. He paused, expecting to hear an elderly woman's voice waft over the post office boxes. He was surprised by a male voice. His surprise grew at what the voice said.

"Hi. Agent Holden Joyce. FBI. Looking for Chief Sam Mason."

Sam's eyes met Bev's, and he saw his own question mirrored in hers.

The FBI? This couldn't possibly be good.

CHAPTER SEVENTEEN

Holden Joyce's polished black dress shoes squeaked on the marble floor as he rounded the post office boxes. He was in his midfifties, about Bev's age, with salt-and-pepper hair. Tall but fit in his blue suit. Sam could tell right away he was the kind of guy who liked his job enough to be an asshole about it.

Holden glanced around, a smirk on his face. "Quaint little place you've got here."

The sarcastic tone in his voice was duly noted.

Lucy must have caught the tone too, because she eyed him skeptically from her spot under the window, her lip curled in a slight snarl. She didn't even bother to get up to greet him, as if he weren't worth the effort.

"Can I help you?" Sam asked.

"Holden Joyce. FBI." The man extended his hand

and they suffered through a round of tense intro-
ductions.

When he got to Bev, he said, "Nice to see you
again, Sheriff Hatch." But the tone of his voice didn't
sound as though it was nice to see her again.

"So what brings you here, Joyce?" Bev asked. By
the tone of her voice, it wasn't nice to see him again
either. Sam guessed Bev had had dealings with this
Joyce and they hadn't been particularly pleasant.

"Murder," Holden said. "We've got a dead officer
and a dead mayor tied together by a fingerprint from a
dead body."

Bev folded her arms over her chest. "So, what's the
FBI's interest?"

Joyce glanced out the window. "Murder across
state lines."

Sam frowned. Holden was lying. The FBI was
usually into bigger things. But considering that this all
had to do with a drug-dealing ring, Sam shouldn't be
surprised the FBI had come. But shouldn't it be the
Drug Enforcement Agency that descended on them?
The way Holden was looking around the squad room
made him think there was much more to this.

Sam glanced at Tyler's old desk, now Wyatt's desk.
Now that the FBI was involved, everything about
Tyler would come out. As far as Tyler's reputation, let

the chips fall where they might. Sam was more worried about what else the FBI agent would dig up.

"I've never known you to be interested in that," Bev said.

Joyce simply raised a brow at her. "We're interested in lots of things. Speaking of which, I need everything you have on the Tyler Richardson case."

Sam locked eyes with Jo. Things were getting worse fast. Sam had just started building a rapport with Bev, and he hoped she might understand why Sam and Jo would want to protect Tyler if certain things came to light. Sam doubted Holden Joyce would be as understanding.

"I've got that case covered," Bev said.

"Not anymore."

Bev frowned. "What do you mean? Are you taking over the Dupont case? Is that why you're interested in Richardson?"

"No." Holden said. "My interest is in the Scott Elliott murder. But I'm authorized to collect any information that might be pertinent to it. I think that because Scott Elliott's fingerprint was found at the murder scene of Officer Tyler Richardson and Mayor Dupont, I might need to look over your notes on those two cases."

Sam could tell that Bev was pissed. She glared at

Holden. "I have the Richardson stuff back at the sheriff's office. Like I said, I've been looking into it."

Holden frowned at Sam. "You don't have anything here?"

Sam shook his head. "No. I gave it to Sheriff Hatch."

Holden looked dubious. "Everything? Maybe you're holding out on Sheriff Hatch."

Bev quirked a brow at Sam.

"What do you mean?" Sam asked. But had a sinking feeling that he knew what Holden Joyce meant.

"Let's just say I think you might have messed with the outcome of a case before. You know the one I mean. Your cousin Gracie."

"That was almost twenty years ago." Sam said. "I was a rookie then. Protecting my cousin."

"Yes, but there're a lot of unanswered questions about what happened to the suspects in that case," Joyce said.

Sam guessed Holden Joyce was old enough to have been in the FBI when his cousin's case came to trial. But the FBI hadn't been involved, so what did Holden know about it? Maybe he was bluffing.

"Wait a minute. What does this have to do with the case we're investigating now?" Bev cut in.

"I'm simply pointing out that Chief Mason's methods of investigation might be a little, shall we say, unorthodox."

Bev held up her hands. "Well, now hold on a minute. I'm investigating too. And as far as I can see, Chief Mason hasn't done anything ... unorthodox. In fact, we're narrowing in on a suspect right now."

Holden cocked a skeptical brow. "Oh? Who? Tell me more about it."

"Well, because you already seem to know everything, you must be aware that Chief Mason was meeting with Mayor Dupont the night of his death because Dupont claimed to have information linking Lucas Thorne to the influx of drugs flooding the county," Bev said.

"So he says," Holden said.

Bev ignored him and continued. "Sam's been building up contacts in the area. One of them told him that drugs are being distributed by a municipal employee. Someone who wouldn't be questioned if they were going to various houses to make drops."

"You mean like a cop?" Holden asked Bev the question, but his eyes remained trained on Sam.

Bev's eyes flicked from Holden to Sam. "Or a garbageman."

"Is that your suspect? A garbageman?"

"Forest Duncan. We have him tied to the case through arrest reports from Tyler Richardson," Sam said.

"So this Forest Duncan, does he drive a black SUV with a roof rack? Because one of your locals saw a truck like that leave the scene, I'm told," Holden said.

How did he know that? Clearly, Holden Joyce already knew more about the case than he let on.

"Well, no. He had a red Pinto in his driveway," Sam said. "But we don't know what other vehicles he has. Maybe he has a black SUV stored away. His house didn't reflect the kind of money that would be coming in for a drug dealer, so we think he's hiding funds somewhere."

Hopefully, that would satisfy Holden Joyce as far as the black truck went.

"So then the only person tied to this case who drives a black SUV with a roof rack is your friend Mick Gervasi."

It felt like a punch in the gut. Crap. How much did this Holden know about him anyway? It was almost as if he were here to nail Sam, using the case as an excuse. Thorne had probably planted people in law enforcement. If Holden Joyce was here on Thorne's request, trying to frame Sam, this didn't bode well.

"Oh, you didn't think we knew about Mr. Gervasi,

huh?" Holden looked smug. "In fact, we know a lot. Especially in connection with what happened during the trial for your cousin."

"I don't see how that's pertinent to the current case," Sam said.

"It is when it indicates how you might handle things that aren't going your way."

Kevin piped in. "Gervasi isn't the only one that drives a black SUV with a roof rack. I've been researching, and I've narrowed it down, but there're more than one thousand SUVs in the area with roof racks. And it could be someone who isn't even from the area."

Was Kevin stalling for time, protecting Mick? Sam's estimation of the officer rose a few notches.

"I'm getting a little confused here," Bev said. "Are you accusing Chief Mason of something?"

Holden looked contrite. "No, of course not. I'm simply stating the facts."

Holden held Sam's gaze for a few tense seconds before turning to Bev. "If you're almost done here, I'll follow you to your office and pick up what you have on the Richardson case."

Bev scowled. Sam could tell she didn't really want Holden Joyce following her to her office, but what choice did she have?

"Fine. We're done here." They walked off, Bev giving Sam a glance on her way out.

Sam could tell that Bev didn't like Holden Joyce. At least that was one saving grace. Bev would be on his side. But he also knew he'd better prove who the killer was fast, because Bev wouldn't remain on his side if she discovered he'd been lying.

BY THE TIME Kevin clocked out of work that day, he had a major tension headache. The visit from the FBI agent had been disturbing, especially the allegations he'd tossed around about Sam. Kevin was under no illusion that Sam was some angel, but what had he done in the past? Judging by the FBI agent's threat, he knew it had been something bad.

It didn't matter what Sam had done in the past. Kevin knew he was the kind of guy who did the right thing *now*. And besides, Sam had said something about protecting his cousin. Protecting family was the right thing to do. That FBI guy was working some angle, and Kevin wasn't going to stand by and let him railroad Sam.

That was why he'd spoken up about the black SUVs. He figured it probably was Mick's truck that

Rita had seen, but he wanted to do his part and throw the FBI guy off track. He'd been nervous that Wyatt would throw his two cents in, but he'd kept his mouth shut. Kevin might have to reevaluate his impression of the guy. At least Wyatt had his loyalties in the right place and sided with his own team instead of blabbing to the FBI.

It almost seemed as though the FBI guy was trying to pin the murder on Sam. Had Sam really done something questionable twenty years ago? Did Sam really kill Dupont? But if he had, why would Kevin's contact be trying to get him to lead the investigation to the glove planted on Sam's property? Seemed like they could come up with easier evidence if Sam was the killer.

Kevin's gut churned. When they'd gotten word about Scott Elliott, he'd half hoped Elliott was his contact. But even if he was, Kevin knew the notes wouldn't stop. A new person would take his place. The photo of the guy in the shallow grave cinched it— Elliott wasn't any of the guys that Kevin had met before.

To top it all off, his contact had left another note the night before. Kevin had had a hell of a time wording the reply to persuade them that it wasn't the right time to lead them toward the glove.

And now, if the FBI guy was in cahoots with Thorne, Kevin would have to be extra careful about how he proceeded.

He picked up some aspirin at the convenience store and then drove past the new construction area, keeping his eye on the spot where he'd buried the glove. They were pouring concrete now right next to it. Hopefully, the glove would still be discoverable when he needed it to be, and hopefully, no one else would find it beforehand.

Kevin didn't know how much longer his contact was going to believe his lame excuses. Too bad they were nowhere near locking Thorne up. Maybe this new lead with the garbageman would speed things up.

His thoughts turned to the thumb drive hidden in his kitchen. Was it time to take that out and give it to Sam? What if there was something hidden on it that could help them put Thorne away faster?

He had to be really careful about how he proceeded with that thumb drive, too. How would he explain it being in his possession? He didn't want to ruin his reputation in the police department, nor did he want to lose Sam's trust.

His job was becoming important to him. It had felt good to be trusted to go to the medical examiner and bring back the results of the Elliott autopsy. Maybe he would think about coming on full-time once this case was over. Now he regretted turning down the full-time position that had been offered to him before they'd hired Wyatt.

Not wanting to attract attention, he continued past the construction site to his house, dread gnawing at him. Hopefully, there wouldn't be another note from his contact—or something worse—waiting when he got there.

CHAPTER EIGHTEEN

J o arrived home later than usual that night. The day hadn't gone very well at all. The appearance of Holden Joyce had been a complete surprise and not a pleasant one. The only saving grace was that Bev seemed to be on their side. For now.

As she pulled into her crushed-stone driveway, she spotted a ball of orange fur on her porch. The cat hunched over the dish, eating the food she'd put out before she'd left that morning. Finally, a bright spot in the day.

She got out of the car and approached slowly, not wanting to scare the small cat off. Golden eyes regarded her warily as she sat on the porch step and held her hand out toward the cat, making cooing noises.

The cat's eyes flicked from her hand to the food then to the safety of the woods. It crouched further, ears flattening, ringed tail twitching as if the cat was deciding whether to trust Jo or make a break for it. Was it a boy or a girl? Jo had no idea how to tell the gender of a cat, but she got a sense it was female. Jo sat patiently until, finally, the cat made a cautious move toward her.

"There you go. I won't hurt you."

The cat came closer.

"I'm the one putting the food out. Maybe when winter comes, you'll want someplace warm. You'd better make friends with me," Jo said, already picturing how she might put a cat bed on the porch, maybe even inside when the temperatures dipped below freezing.

Mew.

The cat sniffed her fingers, and Jo tentatively reached out an index finger to lightly scratch its head. The cat stiffened but didn't run away. Her fur was soft and silky.

She'd finally worked her way around to scratching the cat's neck, and the cat had even rubbed her face against Jo's knee a few times when the crunch of tires on crushed stone interrupted them. She looked up to see the White Rock Police Station Tahoe pulling in with Sam behind the wheel, Lucy staring out the front window.

The cat stiffened.

As Sam came to a stop, the cat pulled away and raced into the woods.

"You got a new friend?" Sam asked, his eyes following the path of the cat as it bounded past Jo's picnic table.

Jo stood, brushing off her jeans. Orange fur clung to her knee where the cat had rubbed against it. "Stray cat I've been feeding."

Lucy trotted over, wagging her tail, happy to see Jo, then stopped short at sniffing her knee where the cat had been rubbing. She looked up at Jo, her forehead wrinkled and her upper lip curled.

"I guess Lucy doesn't like cats," Jo said.

"Probably jealous," Sam answered.

Jo bent down and scratched behind Lucy's ears. "Don't worry. You're still my favorite." She tilted her head to look up at Sam. "So what brings you by? Break in the case?"

Sam shook his head. "Nah, I just wanted to get your take on Holden Joyce."

Jo sighed and stood. "For that, I think we're going to need some beer."

Sam followed her to the door. Lucy had beat them

to it and was standing at the door, tail wagging, casting disapproving glances at the empty cat bowl. She didn't stray over to the bowl, though. Most likely, she was anticipating the bacon-flavored dog treats that Jo kept in her cupboard.

As they passed through the living room, Jo gestured toward the couch. "Have a seat. I'll get the beer." She proceeded to the kitchen, pulled two beers from the refrigerator, and tossed two treats to Lucy, who caught them in midair.

When she returned to the living room, Jo found Sam perched uncomfortably on the edge of her white-and-pink floral sofa, looking like a child in his Aunt May's fancy living room. Jo almost laughed. Sam definitely looked out of place amidst the shabby-chic muted-florals-and-white-paint decor. He was more of a camouflage-pattern-and-natural-wood-stain kind of guy.

"So, Holden Joyce. What do you think?" Sam asked.

"Hate him. You?"

"Yeah, pretty much." Sam swigged his beer.

Jo leaned back in her chair. "I don't think he likes you very much either. Do you think he really has something on you? I mean, I know about the knife, but Thorne has that, so ..." Jo let her voice trail off. She'd never asked the details about what had happened back then, and Sam had never volunteered. Was that why Sam had come over? He didn't usually just drop by. Maybe he wanted to give her the full story, seeing as Joyce might try to use it against him.

Her eyes drifted toward the bedroom, thoughts of the notes of her sister's disappearance crowding her mind. If Sam was taking her further into his confidence, should she do the same? She could show it all to Sam right now. He might even have some ideas.

She knew Sam would try to help, but she didn't want to distract from the case they were working on. Besides, she was letting her past go. She'd buried her notes at the bottom of a drawer, and that was where they were going to stay. They had more important things to work on.

Sam took a swig of his beer and sat back, his thumbnail scratching at the label as he talked. "Back when that happened to my cousin, she didn't exactly get the justice we were hoping. It was rich kids who did it. Not just one, a bunch of them." Sam paused and looked out the window, the pain he felt for his cousin flickering in his eyes. "Anyway, those kids had parents with deep pockets and attitudes that they could get away with anything. Some of the ringleaders were gonna get off. We went down to try to talk to the weakest link to make sure that the right people were getting punished."

Jo leaned forward, her elbows on her knees. What, exactly, had Sam and Mick done? "And what happened?"

"Nothing. We talked to him. He was scared."

"So how does that translate to the FBI threatening you today?"

"Next day, the kid turned up dead."

Jo relaxed back in her chair. "But the last time you saw him, he was alive?"

Sam nodded and reached down to bury his fingers in Lucy's fur. "He was gonna tell the truth about who the ringleader was. He ended up taking the brunt of the blame, even though he was dead."

Jo pressed her lips together. "That sucks." Now she could see how Sam would have been driven to try to make sure the truth came out, even if it might have taken unorthodox means. He was all about justice, and she knew sometimes following the law didn't result in justice. She couldn't blame him.

"Anyway, seems like Holden Joyce has some assumptions about what went on back then."

"And Thorne has a knife with blood on it that might be misinterpreted as a murder weapon."

Sam nodded. "But there's nothing we can do about

that now. We need to wrap up this case quick, before Holden Joyce has an excuse to dig deeper."

"Do you think Joyce could be working with Thorne?" Jo asked.

"I don't know. Either he's got it in for me, or he's working with Thorne or he has another agenda we don't know about."

Jo looked out the window. The cat lurked at the edge of the woods, crouched down, peering through the trees toward the house. Maybe she would put another bowl of food out for it after Lucy left. She hoped Lucy didn't really hate cats that much because if she adopted it, she didn't want it to be problematic for Lucy to visit.

"What about the FBI looking into Tyler's case?" Jo asked.

Sam blew out a breath. "Yeah, that could get dicey. But once we find Dupont's killer, they'll probably back off on that."

"Okay, we just need to up our game. What else can we do to prove that Forest Duncan is the distributor?" Jo asked.

"I've got Mick looking into the grandson. If he's involved, he probably knew the players. I figure if the grandson can place Duncan with Scott Elliott, then maybe we can get probable cause to do more searching." Sam sipped his beer. "And Bev is looking into his finances. If we find something shady in there, then we can look further."

"Yeah. Luckily, Bev seems to be on our side," Jo said.

"She is now. Mostly, I think she's on the side of justice. I get the impression she doesn't like Holden Joyce very much, but if she suspects what Holden is saying about me is true, she'll switch sides pretty quick."

Sam was right. Jo got the impression Bev didn't put up with anyone trying to con her. Hopefully, she wouldn't find out what they'd done for Tyler, or they might end up with a powerful enemy who could make future investigations difficult. So, they had Holden Joyce against them and Bev tentatively on their side. "What do you think about Kevin and Wyatt? Should we bring them in on everything we know?"

"Maybe Kevin. I got the impression he was stalling for us with that comment he made about Mick's truck."

Jo nodded. She'd thought the same thing. Kevin was turning out to be a valuable ally.

"But I still don't want to include them. Wyatt's too new. I don't have a good feel for him yet, and Kevin, well, sometimes the less you know, the better." Sam chugged down more beer. "Maybe in time, we can let Kevin know what we know, but this could get dicey, and it doesn't seem fair to get him in too deep."

"Hopefully, after this case is over, there won't be anything to let him in on. All this Tyler stuff will be behind us."

"One can only hope," Sam said. "In the meantime, we need to speed things up. We don't want to give Holden Joyce any extra time to dig something up."

CHAPTER NINETEEN

The next day, Sam found himself alone in his office as he contemplated the case. His cell phone, set to vibrate, sat on the desk, awaiting Mick's text. Mick had told Sam he was going to work on Barbara Bartles's grandson. He was positive the guy knew something about who had stolen the car that was at the scene of Tyler's death. Sam suspected Mick's idea of work included a bottle of whiskey. He probably wouldn't be up this early.

Sam eyed the stack of mail on the corner of his desk. He'd been too busy to sort through it. There was usually nothing important in the stack anyway.

Wyatt and Kevin had both gone out on local calls. Even with the murder investigation, the misdemeanors and neighbor disputes still needed tending. Jo was taking care of a fender bender by the Sacagewassett River. Sam was enjoying the peace and quiet—until a shadow in the form of Holden Joyce appeared at his door.

Sam's day was already starting to go downhill.

Sam motioned him in and slid the phone off his desk. He knew people like Holden. They stuck their noses into everything. He didn't need Holden seeing the text from Mick.

He put the phone in his pocket as Holden strutted in, a manila folder in his hand and an arrogant look on his face.

"Have a seat." Sam gestured to the oak chair with the shortened leg. Holden sat, and the chair tipped forward. Holden's brows mashed together. Sam bit back a smile.

"What's the status of this suspect you mentioned yesterday?" Holden leaned back, and the chair tipped again. Again, Sam refrained from smiling.

"I don't have anything new to report so far. It's still early in the day," Sam said.

"Oh, you can't manufacture something?" Holden asked.

Sam leveled a look at the FBI agent. He leaned forward and tapped his index finger on the smooth top of his oak desk to punctuate his words. "We don't work that way around here. Maybe you do that in the FBI, but here, we collect real evidence."

Holden leaned forward too, except when he did, the chair tipped and threw him off balance. A look of anger crossed his face. "What the hell is wrong with this chair?"

Sam sat back, innocence plastered all over his face. "Sorry, it's a little uneven. We got the castoff furniture here. It's all old and broken," Sam said.

"Really? Or is this another example of your unorthodox methods?" Holden tipped the chair back and forth. "Makes the suspect uneasy, doesn't it?"

Sam was just about to reply with a sarcastic remark when Bev Hatch appeared in the doorway.

"I've seen you do worse, Agent Joyce," Bev said.

Holden turned to Bev. "Sheriff Hatch, do you have any light to shed on the case this morning?"

"Not much. Just following up on a few things." Bev came into the room.

Holden stood, hefting the manila envelope in his hand. "Me too."

He flipped open the folder and tossed a few photos on Sam's desk. They were of Sam and Jesse. One of them showed the two meeting behind the auto body shop where Jesse worked earlier this summer. Another was of them meeting in the woods near the campground. Holden tapped Jesse's face with his index finger.

"This guy here is a drug dealer. And this meeting here behind this building looks suspiciously to me like a drug deal." Holden's smug gaze flicked from Sam to Bev, who was frowning at the photos.

"Is that your contact?" Bev asked.

"Yeah. Jesse Cowly. He's a small-time dealer. I've been grooming him so I can get at the bigger fish up the chain." Sam looked at Holden. "You guys do that all the time, right? Pass over the little guy so you can get information. He feeds you what you want to know, and you get a bigger catch."

Bev turned to Holden. "We all do it. I think you're making a big assumption with these photos. Do you have any proof to back it up?"

Holden remained silent.

"He doesn't, because it's not true," Sam said.

"So you say," Holden said. "To me, this looks like a drug deal. And since we got a tip that a municipal employee is dealing drugs, you have the perfect cover. You pass it on to this Cowly guy, and he distributes it."

"Nah. That's not the way it played out, and I think you know it," Sam said.

"We don't know any such thing. How do we know you didn't kill both Mayor Dupont and Officer

Richardson? Our records indicate Richardson might have been into something that has to do with these drug dealings."

Sam was surprised the FBI had such information, but they didn't know the half of it. Richardson had something to do with the drugs, all right. He was in the middle of the whole ring. Sam didn't enlighten him, though. The less Holden Joyce knew, the better.

"Oh, so you've got nothing to say now, huh? And it's no surprise. You've gone rogue before. You and your friend Gervasi. Now it seems you'd have reason to go rogue again, especially if your department is corrupt."

"Now wait a minute." Bev held up her hands. "This is all conjecture and assumption. We're cops. We work with clues and logic." She leveled Holden Joyce with an angry look. "And you know how I hate unfounded assumptions."

"Assumptions are simply theories that need to be proven," Holden said. "Maybe Chief Mason here is trying to frame this garbageman. What kind of a garbageman deals drugs? And the guy lives in a dump. Mason probably has a whole array of people he can use as fall guys here. Maybe Dupont was onto *Mason* and that was what the meeting was about."

Bev's face turned red. "Listen, Joyce. When you

have some physical evidence that proves your accusations, then you come here and give it to us. Until then, this is all just guesswork. I don't think Sam would be working this case like he is if he were the drug dealer."

"We do have one piece of physical evidence," Holden said.

"What's that?" Bev asked.

"The hair that was found inside the chamber of the gun. The only way it could have gotten in there was when the killer was loading the bullets." Holden pointed to Lucy, who lolled in the sunshine, glaring at him. Her ears were straight up on high alert. Her body appeared to be relaxed, but Sam knew she was ready to jump at Holden if he even looked at Sam crossways.

Bev snorted. "Nice try, but that hair won't help you in this case."

Holden scowled. "Why not?"

"It's feline hair. From a cat."

Holden's glare drifted from Bev to Sam to Lucy. He grabbed the photos off Sam's desk and shoved them in the manila envelope. "Be that as it may, don't forget we're working this case hard." He turned to Sam and jabbed his index finger in Sam's direction to punctuate his next words. "And we will get to the real truth."

He turned and stalked out without another word.

Bev stared after him, her arms folded across her

chest. "If I didn't know better, I'd think he's trying to frame you." She turned to Sam, her eyes still narrowed. "Unless his accusations have some foundation in truth?"

Sam shook his head. "No. You already knew I had been grooming Jesse as a contact. That's him in the photos, and the meetings were when he gave me information on drug drops during the summer. You don't think I'm really involved in this, do you?"

Bev studied him hard before she spoke. "Not sure. I know I think Holden Joyce is a blowhard. I've run up against him before. He makes a lot of assumptions. I can't stand the guy."

"That makes two of us."

Bev turned narrowed eyes on Sam again, her voice low and serious. "But that doesn't mean he's always wrong. We'll follow the clues and play it by the book. On this case, we have to do things the right way."

"I wouldn't have it any other way," Sam said, ignoring the vibration of the phone in his pocket. It was probably Mick texting about the grandson, something he didn't want Bev to know about, especially because he agreed to go by the book.

Jo appeared in the doorway, looking over her shoulder to the squad room behind her. "I just passed

Holden Joyce rushing out of here. What's up with him?"

"He's got a hair up his ass," Bev said.

Sam's phone vibrated again as Kevin, Wyatt, and Reese all crowded into the doorway. Great. Just when he wanted to get out of here and read Mick's text, the whole crew was in his office. At least Reese hadn't brought doughnuts. Doughnuts would cause people to linger, and he wanted to get rid of them as soon as possible.

"I don't like that guy," Reese said. "He gave a talk in one of our classes at the academy. What a jerk."

"Yeah, he likes to push his weight around. I know the type," Wyatt said.

"Don't like him either," Kevin added.

It was getting crowded in the office. Sam tried to inch his way toward the door. "It's unanimous none of us like him. But one thing's for sure. He's getting hot on this case."

"Yeah, well, we just have to solve it quickly so we can get him off our backs," Kevin said.

"The key is Forest Duncan. I just know in my gut that he's got something to do with this. All we need is one little incriminating piece of evidence to allow us to uncover the truth about him," Sam said.

"What about his alibi?" Wyatt said. "You said he

was at home, gaming. I have an idea how we might be able to prove otherwise by checking the servers."

Sam's brows rose. "Really? Go for it."

"I'm on my way to Judge Firth with a warrant for his finances," Bev said. "I'm going to personally walk it over and make sure we get it right away. I'm also having my crime scene investigators go over the crime scene photos again to look for physical evidence. I know we've been over it a million times, but you never know what a set of fresh eyes might find."

"Here's his photo that you wanted me to print." Reese handed Sam an eight-by-eleven piece of paper along with the mail, which he added to the growing stack on his desk.

Bev looked over her shoulder. "What's that?"

"A photo of Forest Duncan. It's a long shot, but I just might have a lead that can connect him to Scott Elliott. And if we can do that, then maybe then we can use that connection to get him to talk."

CHAPTER TWENTY

"And just how did Mick get this information?" Jo asked a couple of hours later as they headed toward Nashua in the Tahoe. Jo was a little leery of Mick's methods of extracting information. Beating information out of a suspect wasn't exactly admissible in court, but then again, they probably wouldn't have wanted to admit that they'd used Mick to get to the grandson anyway.

Sam glanced over at her. "Not what you think. Single-malt scotch."

Jo sat back in the seat, relieved, "Oh. That's good. So he admitted to stealing the car?"

"No, not him. He said he helped out his friend."

"And we think this friend was Scott Elliott."

"Right. And now we need to show Danny Bartles

the photos of Elliott and Duncan. Maybe if he thinks he's being linked with a drug ring, he'll be scared into telling us something more."

"Unless he's the leader."

"Nah. Mick said the kid was green. He might be on the fringes, but he's not into anything deep enough."

"So scaring him will get him to tell us what he knows."

"That's the plan."

Jo opened the bag they'd gotten from Brewed Awakening on the way out of town and pulled out a jelly doughnut. "Want one?"

"No."

From the backseat, Lucy whined, and Jo twisted around to look at her. "Not you. These aren't good for you."

"They aren't good for you either," Sam said.

Jo looked down at the doughnut. He had a point. Maybe she'd eat only half. She ripped it in half and took the big section with the jelly and shoved a piece in her mouth.

"How are we gonna tell Bev we came by this information?" she mumbled around the treat.

"We'll leave Mick out of it. We'll say we tied Danny Bartles to the stolen car. It was his grandmother's car, so it's not a stretch, and besides, the suspicion of him having something to do with it being stolen is in our notes from Tyler's initial investigation."

"Yeah, but no one ever followed up on that."

"That's not our fault. We were removed from the investigation. We were told not to look any further, so we didn't. Can't help it if the Staties didn't follow up properly."

"But what if this Bartles guy knows more about Tyler?"

"What if he does?" Sam asked. "We can't stop that now. Tyler was into something bad, and it's probably going to come out."

Jo settled back in her seat, flipped up the plastic tab on the lid of her coffee cup, and took a sip as she looked out the passenger window. The scenery had changed from the mountains and fields of northern New Hampshire to the strip malls and suburban developments of southern New Hampshire.

"Hopefully, we can contain the damage," Sam said.

"I'm really worried about what's in that box."

"If Tyler was working with Thorne, what could possibly be in there?" Sam asked. "Maybe he kept drug-deal records or something. Maybe there's some evidence that can help us put Thorne away."

"Or maybe there's some evidence that makes us look bad. Why would Tyler keep evidence against his own father? Makes more sense that he was building up something against us just in case we discovered what he was up to."

"I guess there's no sense in worrying about it. We still haven't discovered where the box is, and we're the only ones who know about the key. Who needs to even know there was a box?"

"True, but I'd still feel better if we could get to it first. You never know who's going to remember Tyler opening a safety deposit box somewhere. Or the two of us asking about one. It just makes me nervous," Jo said.

Sam didn't respond, but the way his jaw tightened told Jo that he felt the same way.

"What if Bartles won't talk?" Jo asked.

"Don't worry," Sam said, patting his pocket. "I have an ace up my sleeve."

DANNY BARTLES LIVED in a run-down apartment building that smelled of cheap curry, bad body odor, and stale beer. Even Lucy wrinkled her nose as Sam and Jo navigated the corridor to his apartment.

They knocked, and after a few minutes, a guy in his mid-twenties with scraggly hair and bloodshot eyes who was holding a bag of frozen corn to his head answered.

"You Danny Bartles?" Sam asked.

"Huh?"

He stared at them through blurry eyes. It must've taken him a second to realize that Sam and Jo weren't his drinking buddies, and once he did, his eyes darkened with suspicion. "Who are you?"

"We have some questions," Sam said.

Bartles started to shut the door. "I don't think so."

Sam put his foot in the door, and Lucy rushed in while Sam pushed the door open. Bartles stumbled back. "Hey, you can't —!"

Sam put his arm out to steady the man, a smile on his face. "Oh, I'm sorry about that. Didn't mean to push you. Lucy here gets a little excited whenever we bring her to visit someone." Sam gestured toward the dog. "Don't you, girl?"

Lucy practically smiled. Her whole body wagged as if she knew what Sam was up to and she was playing along to put the guy at ease.

"She likes you." Jo smiled at Bartles, also playing along.

Bartles relaxed. Apparently, he wasn't one of their

smarter suspects. That was good. It would make it easier to get information out of him.

Then his eyes narrowed. "Wait, who are you people?"

"Chief Sam Mason." Sam showed his badge, and Bartles stiffened. "Don't worry. You're not in trouble. We heard you might have important information on a case we're working up north. We're not even local, so we have no jurisdiction for anything you might be into down here," Sam said.

"Um, I don't really know anything. You're wasting your time." Bartles started backing up toward the door, reaching for the knob.

"We'd really appreciate the help. And there's a substantial reward if it leads to an arrest."

Bartles stopped at the mention of the reward. Jo glanced at Sam. As far as she knew, there was no reward. But then again, judging by the mismatched furniture, the particleboard bookcase with one shelf hanging down, and the dilapidated state of his apartment, she knew that one hundred bucks would probably be a big reward to this guy. Sam would be happy to pay that out of his pocket if he provided good information.

"Reward?"

"Yup. It's a bundle too."

"What do you want to know?"

"Earlier this summer, your grandmother's car was stolen. You know anything about that?"

Bartles's eyes darted from Sam to Jo to Lucy, a nervous reaction that Jo took to mean he did know something despite the word that came out of his mouth.

"No."

"We hear that Scott Elliott had something to do with it," Sam said.

"Who?"

"I think you know Scott, don't you?"

Bartles shrugged. Apparently, he was either too hung over, or just plain old not smart enough to come up with a lie. "Okay, maybe I know him, but I didn't have anything to do with any car stealing."

"We know that, son," Sam said in his friendliest voice. "Now, I'd like to show you some photos just to make sure we're talking about the same person."

Sam gestured toward the dirty brown-plaid sofa, and Bartles slumped on it while Sam and Jo each took a chair. Lucy sat on the floor between them. Sam tossed a photo of Scott Elliott on the coffee table. It was a nice photo of him with his hair combed back and a smile on his face. Jo didn't know where Sam had gotten it, but it looked like a photo for a work badge.

"Is that the guy?" Sam asked.

"And you say there's a reward for this information?" Bartles asked.

"Yep."

"Yes, that's Scott Elliott. But like I told you, I wasn't involved in anything illegal with him."

Bartles stared down at the photo. He adjusted the package of frozen corn on his head. "Hey, wait a minute. Some guy was asking about the stolen car and Elliott last night in the bar."

"Oh really?" Sam asked.

Bartles frowned. "I'm not getting in the middle of anything bad, am I?"

"Nope, not at all. No one will know you spoke to us."

Bartles's frown deepened. "Well, if no one knows I talked to you, how can I collect the reward?"

"It's all done anonymously," Sam assured him.

"Okay. Well, I haven't seen Scott in a while anyway."

Sam glanced at Jo. No surprise there. Scott was dead. Apparently, Bartles didn't know that.

"Did he mention anything about the car? Or where he was going with it?" Sam asked.

Bartles adjusted the bag of corn again and looked down at his bare feet. "Nope."

It didn't take a degree in psychology to know that Bartles was lying. Even Lucy could tell, as evidenced by the way she glanced up at Jo.

Sam took out another photo, this one of Forest Duncan, and placed it on the coffee table. "Do you know him?"

"No, man. Why are you asking about all this?"

"And you don't know about anything else that Scott Elliott was into?"

"No. Like I said, I only told him where Gram kept the keys. It's not like I went with him or was into anything that he was into."

"Well, you must have known him pretty well to tell him where your grandmother kept the keys," Sam prodded.

Bartles's eyes darted from Sam to Jo as he realized he'd messed up. He jiggled his leg nervously, the frozen-corn package crunching as his hand tensed on it. "No, I didn't know anything."

"Really? Because if you don't tell us what you know, you could be in deep trouble, and I don't mean with the cops." Bartles's eyes jerked from the photos on the table to Sam.

"Huh?"

Sam tossed another photo on the table, this one of Scott Elliott in the shallow grave.

Bartles's eyes widened. He jumped up from the chair, the freezer pack thudding to the floor. "Shit! What happened to him?"

"Someone killed him. Guess he knew too much. Now, don't you want to make sure we find the person who did this and put him away before he thinks *you* might have known too much?" Sam asked.

"Okay. Shit." Bartles paced the room nervously, the freezer pack thawing on the floor, forgotten. "Okay. I did some stuff with Scott. We hotwired a few cars. But I swear I didn't get into anything that would get anyone killed. And I swear I don't know that guy in the other picture."

"But you must've known something about what Scott Elliott had going on?" Sam leaned back in the chair, as patient as ever. "Come on, Danny, we know you guys all talk."

"I don't know anything. I swear." Bartles continued pacing before he stopped in front of the coffee table. "Well, he did have something going on up north. I have no idea what, but by the way he talked, it was something big. I was trying to cut my association with him because ..." He pointed at the photo of Elliott in the shallow grave. "Well, you know, because I didn't want to end up like that."

"Drugs?" Jo asked.

Bartles shrugged. "He didn't talk much about it, but probably."

"So how do you know it was someone up north?" Sam glanced at Jo.

"One day, we were driving around, looking to score some pot, and he got a weird call."

"From who?"

"No idea, but he U-turned and got all serious about following some guy. Said he was a cop from up north." Jo straightened in her seat. Even Lucy came to attention, sensing that this was important.

"A cop? What was his name?" Sam asked.

"I don't know."

"When was this?"

"I don't know. Beginning of summer."

"Well, what did you do? Did you meet up with him?" Had Tyler been distributing drugs down here?

"No, it was weird. We followed him, but it must have been a wild goose chase because all he did was go into Penny's Peak Ski Area."

"Why? Did he drop something off or meet someone? Why were you following him?"

Bartles shrugged. "I guess he just wanted to see what he was up to."

Jo glanced at Sam. This didn't make much sense. If

Tyler was working with Scott Elliott, why would he have been secretly following him?

"What did you see?"

"Nothing. That's why it was weird. The ski area's closed. It's summer. But I guess the cop must've just been hungry, because he got out and went to the vending machines."

"Was the cop tall with dark curly hair cut just below his ears?" Jo asked.

"Yeah, that's the guy!"

She locked eyes with Sam. She'd just described Tyler Richardson.

"Scott seemed really disappointed that the cop hadn't done anything more than get a candy bar. I wasn't sure exactly what he was expecting, but by that time, I knew he was into some weird shit, and I didn't want to get into it. I figured the less I knew, the better," Bartles slumped back down on the couch. "You don't think the people who killed him are going to come after me, do you?"

"Nah, I don't think so. We'll make sure they don't," Sam said. "Can you tell me where the ski area is?"

"Yeah." Bartles seemed more than eager to help them now, probably wanting the cops to put the bad guys away before he ended up in a shallow grave. "It's right off of exit eight, about two miles to the east. You can't miss the signs."

"Okay, thanks." Sam got up, and Jo and Lucy followed him to the door.

Just before they stepped out into the hallway, Bartles yelled, "Hey, what about my reward?"

Sam turned around and looked at him. "Don't worry. We'll mail it to you."

They stepped into the hall and made a beeline for the Tahoe.

CHAPTER TWENTY-ONE

The ski hill wasn't hard to find. The dirt parking lot was empty. The tall metal terminals and cables of the chairlift cut a path up the hill. Sam figured they put the chairs away at the end of the season. In the winter, the place would bustle with skiers in colorful snow gear, but now it was so quiet you could practically hear the grass grow.

The mountain was simply an overgrown hill compared to what Sam was used to up north, but for skiers who didn't want to drive the extra few hours to the Canadian border, this was a fairly popular place to ski. There was a nice lodge at the top, also closed for the season. Here at the bottom was a building that sheltered vending machines. "This must be where Tyler stopped," Jo said.

"We don't know for sure that it was Tyler." Sam followed her to the building. The vending machines were set under a roof with the sides open. A few machines were visible from the parking lot, but as they got closer, Sam saw the row extended out of sight to the corner of the building.

"No, but it's a pretty big coincidence he fit Tyler's description. And he was from up north."

"What do you think he'd be doing here at the vending machines?" Sam asked. "And do you really think Bartles was telling us the truth?"

Jo nodded. "I didn't see any indication he was lying. He seemed too scared. And besides, it was pretty clear he's small time. He wouldn't have any reason to lie because he wasn't into anything too big."

Sam had thought the same, but it was nice to know Jo agreed. He looked behind the vending machines while Lucy sniffed around the sides. Nothing looked out of place. Just normal everyday vending machines. Jo stood in front of them, looking at the selections.

"It looks like they have Mounds bars. Those are my favorite," she said.

"I'm an Almond Joy man, myself." Sam turned and glanced back at the empty parking lot as Jo fed in money for the candy bar. "Doesn't look like this place gets a lot of use in summer."

Jo reached in and pulled out the candy bar, unwrapped it, tore off the end, and handed Sam half. "I hope it isn't stale."

Lucy, who had made her way around the corner, trotted back, tail wagging.

"Chocolate is bad for dogs," Jo said, her mouth stuffed full.

But Lucy wasn't begging for food. She nudged Jo's hand and then trotted back to the other side of the building, past the last vending machine.

"Wonder what she wants," Sam said as he followed her.

Bathrooms were on the other side of the building, one door for men and one for women.

Jo cracked the ladies' room door. "I'm surprised they don't lock these in the off-season."

Lucy trotted toward the men's room, and Sam followed. Sam opened the door, and Lucy pushed her way inside as he fumbled for a light switch.

The bathroom was done in plain white tile. It smelled a little musty but was fairly clean, which surprised Sam. He would have thought that people would come here to party in the summer and leave a mess. Sure, there was some graffiti on the steel-gray stall dividers, and one of the shower curtains in the stalls at the end had been ripped halfway down, but otherwise, it wasn't too bad.

Lucy had trotted past the showers, and Sam's eyes followed her, his heart skipping when he saw what was next to the shower stalls. Four rows of small lockers, all with their doors open ... except one.

"Are you seeing what I'm seeing?" It was so quiet that Jo's muffled voice could be heard even in the next bathroom.

Sam nodded. "Yeah. Lockers. And one of them has a lock on it."

The door opened, and Jo came in beside him. "These bathrooms aren't in full view of the parking lot. Someone following Tyler here might not have known he came in the bathroom. If they stayed in their car and watched him from a distance, they might have thought he was just getting something from the vending machines."

Sam already had the padlock in his hand and the key out of his pocket. He met Jo's eyes.

"Here goes." Sam put the key in and turned it. The lock slid open with a click.

He removed the lock, pulled the door open, and reached inside, his fingertips brushing against a cold metal box. He pulled it out. It was a lockbox about the size of a notebook and four inches thick.

"Guess we're finally going to get to see what Tyler had hidden away."

JO WATCHED as Sam balanced the box on the sink and unsnapped the metal latch then lifted the lid. "Hopefully, there's something in here that links Forest Duncan to Thorne."

Inside sat a spiral notebook and some photographs. Sam picked up the notebook, and Jo took the photos.

On the second photograph, she hit pay dirt. It was Forest Duncan. "Here's one of Duncan." Her pulse picked up speed as she studied the image, but something wasn't right. The photo wasn't of Forest doing anything illegal, unless you considered crouching in the woods with binoculars illegal. It had a time stamp on the corner, and she shuffled through the others and came to another photo with the same time stamp, but this one was of Scott Elliott unloading boxes from the back of a truck. Drugs?

She put the two photos side by side. They were grainy, and it was hard to make out, but it looked as if the two had been taken in the same spot, just from different vantage points. Had Forest Duncan been spying on Scott Elliott? And why take a photo?

Presumably, Tyler had put the photo in the box. Why would he want a photo of Forest Duncan spying on Thorne's henchman? Was Tyler trying to prove to Thorne that Duncan was trying to get evidence against him? Why keep it in the box? Why not show Thorne right away? And if Tyler had let Thorne go on all those police calls, didn't that mean they were working together?

"Something doesn't add up." Sam frowned down at the notebook.

"Yeah. Tell me about it. Look at these photos. It's almost as if Tyler was spying on Forest Duncan. Or Thorne." Jo showed Sam the images.

"Yeah. This notebook is in some kind of shorthand or code, but there's definitely dates, and I think the coded parts are locations."

Jo studied the notebook over his shoulder. "Some of those dates are days that Tyler let Forest off on some of those police calls."

"No kidding. I'm getting a funny feeling about this."

"Me too." As Jo looked further into the pile of photos, her unease grew. And then she spotted something shockingly familiar. Beech trees with the lower branches broken, just like those she'd seen near the graves linked to her sister's case.

She struggled to breathe as she stared at the photo. It couldn't be. After years of looking, was this finally the spot? Had Tyler captured this inadvertently while spying on Thorne? But where exactly was it?

She looked for landmarks. Nothing. It was just another photo of Scott Elliott. This time, he was carrying a crate in the woods. The more she looked at it, the less sure she was that the beech trees were even marked in the same style. Maybe it was just wishful thinking. Maybe it was —

"What the heck?" Sam's voice interrupted her thoughts. He'd grabbed some papers from the bottom of the box, and he handed them to Jo. She dropped the photo back into the box before taking the papers.

Her heart twisted as she read them. They were blackmail letters demanding money. She glanced up at Sam. "Tyler was blackmailing someone?"

"Yeah. Thorne. And I think I know why." Sam handed her another piece of paper—DNA test results. Jo couldn't believe her eyes. The scrap that Dupont had clutched in his dying hand hadn't told the whole story. Yes, Thorne was the father of a Richardson, but not *Tyler* Richardson. Thorne was the father of Tyler's sister, Clarissa.

They'd had it all wrong.

"The blackmail was for her treatments. That's

where the large deposit of money in his bank account came from."

"And earlier deposits, I suspect. We never looked any further into his account," Sam said. "I always wondered how he afforded those expensive treatments for Clarissa, even after moving in and consolidating bills with his mother. Cops don't make very much."

"But what about all these photos and the dates and locations recorded in the notebook?" Jo asked. "Why would any of this intimidate Thorne? Why would he care if anyone knew he was Clarissa's father?"

"Well, Harry did say that Thorne's wife was a force to be reckoned with, and her family is quite wealthy. That's how Thorne was financed." Sam thought for a minute. "Clarissa was much younger than Tyler. Thorne would have been married when she was born, so he must have had an affair with Mrs. Richardson."

"Seriously?" Jo made a face. "You expect me to believe Thorne would be afraid to let his wife find out he had an affair that resulted in a child?"

"Maybe not so much the wife, but the wife's family money. Didn't Harry say something about a prenup?"

"But wouldn't Thorne make plenty with his drug trade? Why would he care about the wife's money?"

"Maybe he launders the drug money through the

properties he's building. If the wife's family financed it, they could pull the rug out from under him. Without that, he'd have no way to launder the drug money," Sam said. "You have to admit this explains a lot. It's all here. And Thorne did give Tyler money."

"I suppose so. Tyler must have been trying to get something else besides Clarissa to hold over Thorne as extra insurance. That's why he has all these photos and records."

Jo's mind drifted to the photo of the beech trees. It was probably just a coincidence. Maybe the branches weren't cut the same way. She'd have to compare them to the photos she had in the bottom drawer of her armoire later. But even if they were, she had no way to figure out where the area was ... unless Forest Duncan remembered. She took a deep breath and pushed the thoughts to the back of her mind. She had put her sister's case away for good, and what they were working on now was more important. It deserved her full attention.

"But why didn't Tyler tell us?" Jo asked.

"How could he? Blackmailing the resident drug lord isn't exactly something you tell your fellow cops," Sam said. "You know how important his family was to him. His sister always came first. And even though he wouldn't have wanted to go behind our backs like this, he did it for her."

It was true. Tyler had thought the world of his sister. Jo probably would have thought the world of hers.

"And I don't think he ever would have told us, because he wouldn't want Thorne to be put away," Sam said. "If Thorne went to jail, the blackmail money would dry up."

"But what about all these photos and notes? It looks like he was gathering evidence."

"I think he needed to get as much as he could on Thorne to keep blackmailing him in case the threat of telling his wife wasn't viable anymore." Sam picked up the photo of Forest. "And these photos served another purpose. They protect Forest Duncan. Tyler must have had Forest informing on him. That's what all the calls about Forest being let go were about. He had to make it look like he was arresting Forest so Thorne wouldn't think they were working together. He probably had Forest doing odd jobs for Thorne, maybe even dealing drugs, but these photos prove that Forest was working with Tyler." Sam looked at Jo. "Tyler did this to protect Forest."

Jo had mixed feelings. She could understand why Tyler had done what he'd done, but she wasn't sure she could justify him letting Thorne continue his dirty business.

"That would be just like Tyler to make sure Forest didn't get caught up in this whole thing." Jo looked down at the photo then back up at Sam. "But if Forest Duncan isn't the distributor or the one who killed Dupont, who is?"

CHAPTER TWENTY-TWO

S am and Jo stopped at Jo's long enough to drop off the box and for Jo to put out more food for the orange cat, which was waiting on her porch again. Lucy didn't seem keen on the cat's presence, so they left her in the Tahoe.

There was no benefit in telling anyone else about the box. None of the photos showed Thorne in a compromising position, and they already knew Scott Elliott was involved. Having to explain how they'd had possession of the key and knew Tyler had hidden a box would be problematic. Besides, now that they'd discovered Tyler wasn't working with Thorne, they were reluctant to blame him. Who could fault him for taking care of his sister?

It was late afternoon by the time they got back to

the station. Bev, Wyatt, and Kevin were all there. Sam had barely had time to process the ramifications of what they'd found in Tyler's box. All this time, Tyler had been gathering his own evidence against Thorne. They were enemies, not allies. It was doubtful he'd been tipping Thorne off to their stakeouts. But then how had Thorne always known what they were up to? Was there someone else in the department that had been ratting them out?

Bev looked at Sam, suspicion flickering in her eyes. "Where have you been?"

"Following a lead that had to do with Tyler's stolen car."

"Connected to this case?" Bev's eyes flicked from Sam to Jo. "Did it pan out?"

"Unfortunately, no," Sam said. "What about you?"

"I didn't find anything suspicious in Forest Duncan's finances." Bev seemed a bit less friendly, uneasy. Was it because Forest Duncan was turning into a dead end, or had she discovered something else?

Sam glanced at Jo. Now that they knew Forest Duncan probably wasn't working with Thorne, he realized it had been a mistake to build him up as their prime suspect. They needed to figure out another angle and get Bev off Duncan's trail fast. Who knew what she would turn up about him and Tyler?

"I'm not surprised you didn't find anything," Wyatt said. "I checked out Duncan's alibi. He was at home, playing video games, when Dupont was murdered, just like he said."

"Really? Is that irrefutable?" Bev asked.

"He plays a group game. You know, the kind where you can play with other people online. A server keeps track of when they're on. According to his server, he played for four hours that night. He couldn't have killed Dupont."

Kevin frowned. "Couldn't that be faked? He could have had a friend play for him."

"He could have, I suppose," Wyatt said.

Sam seized the opportunity. "We haven't found anything else linking him. Maybe Duncan isn't our guy."

"Sure, maybe. But who else do we have to go with?" Bev asked.

"Maybe we should be looking a little closer to home." Holden Joyce came around the post office boxes, his fist clenched around some papers. Sam wished he'd stopped to take an aspirin. Holden Joyce was the last thing he needed right now.

Joyce folded his arms over his chest, the papers crinkling as he stared at Sam. "Let me guess: your lead didn't pan out."

"No."

"I'm not surprised. I think maybe there's more to this than you're telling us. I dug up a witness who says he saw Officer Harris at the mill long before your official report states."

"Of course I was there," Jo said. "We needed to go there beforehand to make sure we weren't being set up."

"Well, your report doesn't state that."

"An oversight," Jo said. "We were treating it very carefully in case things didn't pan out. We didn't want Thorne to find out the mayor had ratted him out. Could be dangerous for him."

"Yeah, turns out it was dangerous for him anyway," Holden snarled.

"This might be my fault," Kevin volunteered. "I talked to the neighbor who saw Jo, but I didn't report it. I just figured it had already made its way into the report. Sorry."

Sam studied Kevin. Was he telling the truth? If so, why didn't he mention it before? Either way, one thing was clear: Kevin was covering for them.

"Just what are you getting at, Joyce?" Bev demanded.

"A lot of things don't add up about this case," Holden said. "Reports that aren't filled out correctly.

Sam's buddy happening to have an SUV exactly like the one a witness saw speeding away from the murder site. Oh, and the handwriting expert says Tyler Richardson didn't write that last entry in his log." Holden stepped closer to Sam. "So tell me, Chief Mason, what exactly are you up to?"

Sam's fist tightened, and he stepped away from Holden, mentally counting to three before he answered.

"He's not up to anything," Jo said before Sam reached two. "You know as well as we all do that reports don't always get filled out correctly. Sometimes we have to fill in logbooks for each other."

"Yes, but not after one of us is dead." Holden Joyce turned to Sam. "If you confess now, we can cut you a deal. Tell us everything—what you've been up to and why you've been fixing these cases."

"I haven't been up to anything, Agent Joyce."

"Really? There're a lot of inconsistencies, not to mention the little matter of some extra money that showed up in Tyler Richardson's account."

Sam pressed his lips together. When he had thought that Tyler was working with Thorne, he was willing to let the chips fall as they might. Tyler had made a deal with the enemy, and if his reputation was tarnished because of it, then so be it. Now that he knew the extra money was to pay for Clarissa's treatments, he wanted to defend Tyler. But how?

"Yeah, that's right. Your suspect didn't have any extra money, but your cop did. Could that be drug money?" Holden asked.

"I don't see what this has to do with Chief Mason," Bev said. "If Officer Richardson was on the take, you can hardly blame the other cops in the squad."

"Except Chief Mason has been doing things on the side to obscure the facts in the Richardson case, haven't you?"

"No. Our fellow officer was murdered. Of course we're going to look into who did it and try to bring them to justice."

"Still not willing to talk? Then let's not forget about the matter of the money you tried to launder."

Sam's brows creased. "What?"

Holden held the papers up like a trophy. "Through your own slain officer's mother. You should be ashamed."

"No, it wasn't like that," Jo came to his defense.

"So it's no coincidence that Tyler Richardson's mother got the exact same sum of money from the Fallen Officers Fund that mysteriously appeared and then disappeared from Mason's bank account?" Holden Joyce pointed to a copy of a deposit slip on one of the papers. "Funny thing is, there is no Fallen Officers Fund."

Bev's scowl deepened the more Holden talked. She squinted at the evidence, suspicion darkening her eyes. "Now, wait a minute. This doesn't exactly make sense. He wouldn't launder money through his own bank account."

"Maybe. But you have to admit Chief Mason is up to something shady."

Bev pursed her lips, looking from Holden to the evidence to Sam. Sam could tell he was losing her support, but he had no way to clear himself.

"I think it's best that the FBI takes over everything involved in this case," Holden said.

Bev whirled on him. "Now, you wait a minute, Joyce. I'm in charge of the Dupont case. It's a local case. You can butt out. I don't like anyone horning in on my cases."

Holden scowled down at her. "You always were hard to work with, Hatch. If you align yourself with Mason, you might end up getting burned too. Just think about that before you decide whose side you're on."

With that, he pivoted on his heel and stormed out of the squad room.

Sam turned to Bev. "Thanks a lot, Bev. I really appreciate —"

Bev held up her hand. "Shut it, Mason. I just couldn't let that smug asshole take the case. But I'll tell you one thing: everything he's saying doesn't look very good for you."

"I know, but there's an explanation."

"Explanation or not, there're been a lot of inconsistencies, and I think you might have pushed the envelope a few times on this case. I'll give you the benefit of the doubt just this once because somehow, I still think you're a good guy. Not to mention I owe your granddad."

"Appreciate that."

"I'm not sure what Joyce is up to. I don't trust him. This business about giving money to Officer Richardson's mother doesn't make any sense to me. Otherwise, I'd cut my losses and ban you from investigating this case right now." Bev looked around at Jo, Kevin, and Wyatt. "Your people seem to like you and stick up for you. That says a lot about a person. But I'm not stupid, and I don't like having the wool pulled over my eyes. So you've got twenty-four hours to come up with a real suspect in this case before I turn the spotlight on you."

KEVIN SAT at his granite breakfast bar, fiddling with the thumb drive he'd taken from Tyler Richardson's belongings as he considered his options. He didn't like the way things had gone down at the police station earlier that afternoon. He'd wanted to stay and help with the investigation, but Sam had sent him home. He said he'd already logged enough time, and the weary look on Sam's face had told him not to argue.

But now, sitting at home, Kevin worried. It appeared that Holden Joyce really had it in for Sam. And Kevin knew that Sam hadn't gone exactly by the book on a few things. If Joyce wanted to nail him, he probably could. Kevin couldn't let that happen. Especially because some things might be his fault.

If he gave the thumb drive to Sam, it would be an admission that he'd gone against him. That he'd sold out the department for money. Kevin didn't even know if anything could be recovered from the thumb drive, but what if some data on it could help Sam? It might be the only way Kevin could make things right. That and the bloody glove.

He'd have to figure out a way to give it to Sam when no one else was around, because whatever was on it might as easily get Sam into trouble as it could get him out of it. He wouldn't be surprised if Sam was still at the station, puzzling over the case. He could take a ride by and see if the lights were on. But if he did hand it over, he'd risk losing Sam's trust.

Maybe if he told Sam about the bloody glove, that could somehow make up for the way he'd been going behind his back. He'd protected Sam by digging up the glove and putting it somewhere that might incriminate Thorne. Sam could hardly blame him for that, could he? Especially when Sam didn't go by the book all the time himself.

It didn't matter. It was the right thing to do. Kevin shoved the thumb drive in his pocket and headed out to his car. Hopefully, he could catch Sam at the station alone and finally get this off his conscience.

CHAPTER TWENTY-THREE

Sam and Jo stood looking at the corkboard in his office, the smell of the greasy takeout burgers they'd had for supper cloying the air. It was dark. Lights from the shops sprinkled around the common glittered outside the windows. A few tourists and locals leisurely strolled the sidewalks. Inside, the atmosphere was tense.

"We must be missing something," Sam said.

"What about the cat hair?" Jo said. "It's the only physical evidence we have. Maybe we should get a list of everyone who got rabies shots for their cats."

"It's something to try, but I imagine a lot of people have cats, and not all of them keep them up-to-date on their shots. Won't narrow it down much. I think we need to talk to Forest Duncan again. We'll have to tip our hand and let him know that we know he was working with Tyler. That'll put us on the same side. He won't be as nervous, and he might have some information we can use."

"Or he might be afraid the same thing that happened to Tyler will happen to him."

"I still can't believe Tyler was blackmailing Thorne all along," Sam said. "I feel bad that we assumed the worst of him." Sam pushed the stack of mail aside and leaned his hip on the corner of his desk.

"Who could blame us?" Jo asked. "Of course, now Bev Hatch will assume the worst of us."

"Not us," Sam said. "Me."

"But Holden Joyce was onto that log forgery. So I'm in this as deep as you are."

"No. I'll say I forged it."

Jo scowled at him. "I'm not letting you get in trouble for me. I forged the logbook, and I'll own up to it —"

Jo broke off at the sound of the lobby door opening. "Please tell me that's not Holden Joyce coming back," she muttered.

"Hey, Sam." Kevin's voice drifted in from the lobby a few seconds before his face appeared in the doorway. His eyes flicked from Sam to Jo, showing his surprise to find them both there. He shoved something back into his pocket. His keys, Sam assumed. "I saw the light on and thought I'd stop in. Thought maybe you could use some help. You going over the case?"

"Yeah. Thanks for stopping in. I guess we might have to pull an all-nighter."

Sam was impressed that Kevin had taken the initiative to stop in. It seemed he really wanted to help with the case. He'd changed a lot from the lazy officer who only wanted to work the minimum hours he'd been assigned at the start of the summer. Sam wondered if they should share more of the details with him. But not now. Maybe later, after the case was solved. Right now, he didn't want Kevin's mind clouded by all the subterfuge that had gone on behind the scenes.

"So what have you got? We need to get this FBI guy off our backs." Kevin stared at the corkboard.

"You can say that again," Sam said.

"I wonder about Scott Elliott's friends," Jo said. "Maybe we should tackle it from that angle. If he was involved in the drug ring and the murders, maybe one of his friends was too."

"Well, we do need a new angle and new lead," Sam agreed.

Kevin's hand hovered over his pocket. He seemed hesitant. "Yeah, maybe —"

"Hello? Anyone home?"

Harry Woolston appeared in the doorway. "I saw the light on and thought I'd come in and see what you were up to. Figured you might be going over the case."

"Yeah. Come on in." Sam motioned Harry into the office. Lucy broke from her spot in the corner and trotted over to Harry. He bent down to pet her. "Late night, huh, girl?"

Lucy wagged her tail in response.

Harry looked at Sam and Jo. "So what have you got? Maybe I can help. You know, I was a pretty good detective in my time."

Sam and Jo exchanged a glance. "We're not coming up with anything on our own, so maybe you can."

"Great!" Harry stood next to Jo. "So I see you ... ahhh ... ahhh ... *achoo!*"

Harry doubled over with the force of his sneeze, grabbing onto the desk and knocking the pile of mail onto the floor.

"So you *are* allergic to Lucy," Sam said.

"No. He didn't sneeze when he was near Lucy." Jo pointed to the orange hairs on her jeans. "It must be the cat hair from the cat from my porch. She was rubbing against my leg earlier."

Harry pulled a linen hanky from his breast pocket

and blew his nose loudly. "That's right. Doc says I'm pretty allergic to cat dander. Glad I'm not allergic to Lucy, though."

Sam bent to pick up the mail.

Harry knelt to help him, his knees creaking and popping. "Dang stuff piles up when you don't tend to it. Why, when me and the missus go to Florida, sometimes they don't stop the mail in time. When we get home, we have a whole pile of it. Never gets to us in Florida."

Sam stood, looking at the letter in his hand. "Wait a minute. The mail." He spun around to face Harry. "You sneezed in here the other day."

"Yeah, so?"

Sam closed his eyes, picturing who had been in the lobby that morning. Wyatt, Reese, Harry, Kevin, and Alvin Ray, the postman. Harry had come in between Wyatt and Alvin. "Does Wyatt have a cat?"

They all looked at each other. Kevin spoke first. "I'm not sure, but I don't think so. He mentioned he liked having Lucy around and was thinking it might be nice to have a pet. The way he was talking, it sounded as if he didn't have any type of pet."

"I thought so," Sam said. "What about Alvin Ray, the postman? Anyone know about him? Harry?"

Harry shook his head. "I don't know. Why are you asking?"

"You sneezed the other day when you were next to Alvin and Wyatt. Lucy was there too. I thought it was because you were allergic to her. But you never sneezed around her before, and you didn't sneeze around her just now."

"I'm fine around dogs. I'm allergic to cat dander," Harry said. "But Jo has a cat. That's why I just sneezed. What's my sneezing got to do with anything?"

Jo shook her head. "I wasn't in the lobby with you guys. I was in the squad room. I remember hearing you all blabbing while I was waiting for you to come in so we could get to work. Besides, the stray cat didn't rub against me that day. He only started coming up on the porch a couple of days ago."

"Reese doesn't have a cat. Sam doesn't have a cat. So if it's not Lucy or Wyatt, then it has to be Alvin Ray who made you sneeze. He must have a cat."

Harry knit his brow. "Okay. Still don't see why that's important, but I don't know about that. That guy is so meticulous about his uniforms. Did you ever notice they are always perfectly pressed? He takes great pride in the way he looks."

"Why does he wear those grungy old sneakers, then?" Kevin asked.

"Sneakers? He usually wears dress shoes. They're always polished to a spit shine," Harry said.

"Not the other day. His sneakers squeaked on the marble in the lobby. That noise sets my teeth on edge." Kevin looked down at his own feet, and his eyes narrowed. "Unless something was wrong with his regular shoes. Mine were ruined from the pigeon drop-pings in the mill where we found Dupont's body. That stuff doesn't come off, and it eats away at the shine."

Sam held up the mail. "And Alvin Ray delivers mail to every house in town. That explains why Scott Elliott didn't have mail at his house."

"I'm not following you on that one," Jo said.

"We thought maybe the fact that the trash hadn't been picked up at Elliott's house pointed to Forest Duncan because he didn't bother to pick up the trash. But that wasn't it at all. If Alvin Ray is the killer, he'd have known there was no reason to deliver mail to Scott Elliott's place because he was already dead."

"Well, it does seem like a lot of things point to Alvin," Harry said. "But what's this business about a cat?"

"Forensics found a cat hair in the gun used to kill Dupont." Sam grabbed his keys. "We need to get over

239

to Alvin Ray's to see if he has a cat. If he does, we need a sample of the hair."

They followed Sam out of the office, Sam giving instructions as they walked toward the front door. "Kevin, you take a separate car. Jo and I will go in and talk to Alvin. You wait around back in case he makes a run for it."

"What about me?" Harry asked. Sam turned to face him. "Harry, I need you to stay here and watch Lucy. This could get dangerous. And Lucy hates cats. I don't want her running around and getting hurt out there."

Harry's face fell in disappointment. "What? I can help."

"Not this time, Harry," Sam called over his shoulder as he rushed out the door.

CHAPTER TWENTY-FOUR

"Now remember, whatever happens, we need this guy alive so he can testify against Thorne if he's involved," Sam said as they pulled up in front of Alvin Ray's modest Cape Cod.

Jo had looked up the address en route. Kevin had parked on the street behind the house so Alvin wouldn't get spooked by two cars. The plan was for Kevin to cut through the yard of the adjacent house to provide backup if needed. They hoped to verify Alvin had a cat and secure a hair sample as unobtrusively as possible. Sam figured that would be easy. Cats shed all the time. All he had to do was pet the damn thing, and he'd have a sample. Then if it matched the one found in the gun, they'd pull Alvin into the station, hopefully for good.

"It doesn't look like he has much drug money," Jo said. The white house and black shutters were freshly painted. Colorful flowers spilled out of flower beds along the front. Not a blade of grass was out of place. It was kept nice but still didn't have anything that exuded money.

"Looks can be deceiving. Let's pretend this is a friendly call and hope he falls for it. We only need to see if he has a cat. If we can match the hair to the one found inside the gun, we'll have substantial proof to pull him in."

Sam grabbed the brass door knocker and tapped it against the red front door. After a few seconds, the door cracked, and Alvin Ray peered out.

He frowned when he recognized who was standing on his doorstep. "What is it?"

"We just have a few questions," Sam said.

Alvin looked uncertain. "It's kind of late."

"I apologize for that, but we're working overtime on the Dupont case. It's pretty important that we find the mayor's killer," Sam said.

"And you think I can help with that?"

"Why don't you let us in, and we'll talk about it?" Sam didn't like the way Alvin was acting. Was it because he was guilty, or was he just nervous about the cops showing up at his door? Whatever the reason, it made Sam tense.

"I was just on my way out," Alvin said.

"Really? Where to?" Jo asked.

"Dinner. So if you can come back tomorrow ..."

"It will only take a minute," Sam persisted. Alvin stared at them for a few beats then opened the door. "Fine. Come in."

Alvin's place was decked out with the finest furnishings. Granite counters, a huge flat-screen television, and leather furniture.

"Nice place. I didn't realize the postmaster's salary was so high," Sam said.

"I save. I don't spend much." Alvin sidled toward an oak sideboard.

"I see ..."

Meow.

Sam's heart skipped as a long black cat slunk into the room and curled against Alvin's leg. Sam glanced at Jo, and they both tensed, their hands hovering around the guns at their hips. "That your cat?" Sam asked.

Alvin's eyes narrowed. "Yeah. So?"

Sam's eyes drifted to the coffee table, where a new shoebox sat. "Something happen to your shoes?"

Alvin didn't answer. Instead, he whipped open the

drawer of the sideboard, pulled out a gun, and jabbed it in Jo's direction. "Why did you people have to come here and be so nosy? Now I have to change my plan."

"Plan?" Sam's hand hovered near his gun, but he couldn't draw. Alvin was already pointing his gun at Jo. If he made a move for his gun, Alvin would shoot her.

"Don't you even think about it," Alvin warned, his eyes narrowing on Sam's hand.

Sam moved his hand away. Better keep Alvin talking. "Why'd you kill Dupont?"

"I had my orders." Alvin laughed. "That's right. We're one step ahead of you and about to take you down."

"But why leave the gun at the scene?" Sam asked.

"I knew you wouldn't be able to stop yourself from tampering with the crime scene." Alvin's eyes glinted. The man was clearly unhinged. "Were you trying to make it look like a suicide? Yeah, I figured you'd try to obscure evidence and eventually dig your own grave by creating evidence against yourself."

Sam caught a movement out of the corner of his eye. It was Kevin outside the window. Hopefully, he'd seen the situation they were in. If it were Sam out there, he'd go around back, pray that the back door was unlocked, and sneak up behind Alvin, whose back was to the kitchen. Hopefully, Kevin would do the same.

"And what about Scott Elliott?" Sam needed to keep Alvin talking, distracting him in case Kevin did sneak in the back as he hoped.

Alvin scoffed. "That candy ass? He got nervous, and I had to stop him from talking."

"What do you mean?" Sam asked. "Did he run when you shot Dupont? We found his print in the woods."

"Nah, he didn't run. We came to the mill in separate cars in case any of those busybody neighbors saw anything. We figured the more cars, the better to make it more confusing. His car was parked down the dirt road at the end of the path. Mine was on Bartlett Street. We came in through the woods and snuck out the same way."

"So you pulled the trigger and took the evidence on Thorne that Dupont had," Sam said.

"Then I left the gun to frame you. I saw you moved it when I noticed the photos at the police station. I figured you would. How stupid."

"What about Tyler Richardson? Did you kill him too?"

"Yeah, that stupid Scott Elliott got real nervous about that one too." Alvin was almost boasting now.

"But Richardson had to be dealt with. He was causing a problem for the big guy."

"Thorne?" Sam asked.

"Maybe. Maybe *I'm* the big guy. Enough talk. Now I need to figure out how to stage this."

"Stage?"

"Yeah. You guys were trying to frame me for Dupont's murder. See, you and Sergeant Harris here killed him. You were all dealing drugs together, along with Tyler Richardson. Corruption in the police ranks. Wouldn't be the first time."

The back door cracked open silently. Kevin slipped inside and tiptoed toward Alvin, his gun leveled at the postmaster's head.

Sam held up his hands. "Now hold on. You don't have to do this. If you tell us everything you know about Thorne, we'll see that you get protection. New name. New job. And you'll go free."

Alvin laughed. "You think I'm going to fall for that? Nope. I have to shoot Officer Harris here and then shoot you with her gun. Make it look like there was some kind of a disagreement between the two of you when you came over to frame me. She shot at you, and I had to shoot her to protect you. Too bad her shot was fatal."

"I don't think so, Alvin. Put the gun down."

Alvin Ray barely flinched when Kevin spoke behind him. He turned just enough to see Kevin holding a gun pointed straight at his head.

"Oh, a third one. Perfect. Now what if you two were in cahoots and the third one found out? Yep. And what if there was a shootout but not because of me? Because one of you found out the other two were working for the bad guys. He'd have to be silenced, right? It wouldn't be too bad if you all ended up dead, especially with each other's guns. Then there'd be no story to believe but mine."

Sam's gut churned. Alvin was crazy if he thought he could pull that off. But the look in his eye told Sam he just might be crazy. "No one will believe that."

"Oh no?" Alvin scoffed. "Just ask Detective Deckard here."

The statement surprised Sam, and he glanced at Kevin. What was Alvin talking about? He was probably trying to confuse him.

"Yeah, that's right. Well, enough talk. Time for Officer Harris to die." Alvin jabbed the gun straight toward Jo, aiming high at the center of her forehead. Sam's heart skipped, his eyes focusing on Alvin's trigger finger.

Sam reached for his own gun. He had no choice. He couldn't let Alvin shoot Jo.

Behind Sam, something crashed through the window. Glass rained down on the floor as a blur of black and brown catapulted between Jo and the gun.

"No!" Kevin lunged between Lucy and Alvin.

Sam's eyes were still glued to Alvin's finger as he brought his own gun up.

Alvin squeezed the trigger as Sam fired at Alvin.

The two gunshots exploded at almost exactly the same time.

THE IMPACT KNOCKED Jo to the floor. Time seemed to both slow down and speed up. Her ears rang from the blasts, deafening her to everything else. The air was spiced with the heavy scent of gunpowder and the coppery smell of blood.

Was she hit? No. She felt no pain, but something heavy lay on her.

She reached down, and her hands sank into soft fur.

Lucy!

The last thing she remembered was Lucy jumping in front of the barrel of Alvin Ray's gun. Was Lucy hit?

The dog scrambled off her, and Jo looked her over

quickly. She appeared to be fine. Then her eyes fell on what lay beyond Lucy. Kevin lay unmoving, a pool of blood spreading beneath him.

"Shit!" Jo raced to Kevin's side and looked for the wound.

Her eyes darted around the room, catching Sam's. He crouched in front of Alvin, his fingertips pressed to the postman's throat. Their eyes locked. Sam shook his head slowly and reached for his phone.

Jo focused on Kevin as she heard Sam call 911. Kevin didn't move. She pressed on the wound in his neck to stop the blood flow.

"Stay with me, buddy," Jo said.

Kevin's eyes fluttered, and his mouth moved as if he wanted to say something, but no words came out. His hand faltered toward his pocket. "Don't move. Just focus on staying alive." Jo pressed on the wound harder, and Kevin's eyes stopped fluttering.

How had he gotten hit? A whine from Lucy brought her memory back. Lucy had crashed through the window between Jo and Alvin. Kevin had jumped in front of the gun to save her and Lucy from getting hit.

As the ambulance sirens split the air, Sam rushed to Jo's side, feeling for Kevin's pulse. "It's faint."

"Oh no." Harry stood above them.

Sam looked at him sharply. "I told you to stay at the station with Lucy."

"I'm sorry, Sam. I just thought maybe I could help out. And now look what's happened. I've ruined everything."

Harry fell to his knees to help with the compression. He nudged Jo gently out of the way. "Press like this. I learned it while I was in the Marines."

While they waited for the ambulance to arrive, Jo felt the weight of all that had happened. Everything they'd worked for had been for nothing. Alvin wouldn't be able to tell them anything about Thorne, and if her guess was right, Thorne had been smart enough to not have any links linking him to the murder or to Alvin. They'd look, but she doubted they'd find anything.

Kevin was bleeding too rapidly.

As if sensing the gravity of the situation, Lucy had remained off to the side. She inched forward, resting her head on Kevin's thigh, careful to stay out of their way. She whined and looked up at Kevin, her whiskey-brown eyes darting from his face to Jo's.

Jo hoped Kevin wasn't beyond feeling the comfort of Lucy's head on his leg.

CHAPTER TWENTY-FIVE

Three days later...

"I'M TRULY sorry about Officer Deckard." Bev Hatch's face was creased with genuine concern. "How's his outlook?"

"Not good, I'm afraid." Sam's voice was scratchy. Jo glanced up at his haggard face. She guessed she didn't look much better. Between processing paperwork, searching Alvin Ray's place for evidence against Thorne, and late-night vigils at the hospital, neither of them had gotten much sleep.

"He's still in a coma. Doctor said he lost a lot of blood and has minimal brain function."

"You guys could have called me in," Wyatt said

from his desk at the other end of the room. He'd been standoffish since that night at Alvin Ray's. Jo wasn't exactly sure why.

"We didn't think there would be any reason for backup. We were just going to talk to him," Sam said.

"Yeah, I get that. But I keep thinking maybe having an extra officer would have prevented one of them from getting shot." Wyatt glanced from Sam to Jo then sighed. "Can't change that now, I guess."

Jo got the impression he was studying them, trying to figure something out. She was overtired and probably reading more into it, but it almost seemed as if he sensed there was more to these cases than they were letting on. Rightly so, because there *was* more. Maybe Wyatt was more perceptive than she had originally thought.

Jo felt huge relief that they'd tied up both Tyler's and Dupont's murders. That meant they wouldn't have to keep covering for the things they'd done. Even though those things were done with good intent, she still didn't like hiding them.

Now there'd be nothing to keep secret. Well, except for Tyler's box, but no one needed to know about that. They could keep that secret safe and still close his case now that everything had come out about Scott Elliott. His fingerprints in the car at Tyler's murder scene and Alvin Ray's confession of how they'd killed Tyler would allow them to close the case.

Everyone was silent for a moment before Bev spoke again. "At least we were able to get the evidence on Alvin. The cat hair was a match. We got it off one of the cat beds. Never did find the cat."

"Probably got spooked by the gunshots and ran off. It's a hollow victory, because I'm sure Ray could have given up more information on Thorne. At least we can prove he was delivering drugs, especially with these mail bins." Sam gestured toward the plastic mail delivery bins they'd discovered in Ray's basement. All of them had false bottoms. That was how he'd been delivering the drugs—a little bit of mail on the top, drugs on the bottom. It was quite ingenious. Ray was the only full-time postal employee, so there was no one to discover he'd doctored the bins.

"But we didn't find anything that led to Thorne," Jo said. After everything that had gone down, not one shred of evidence had surfaced.

"Thorne might be a lot of things, but he's not stupid," Sam said.

"I know you guys think he's linked to this," Bev said. "And I have my suspicions as well. But all the evidence we've collected leads me to believe that it was Alvin Ray and Scott Elliott alone."

"Of course it does," Sam said.

"And now they're both dead and can't talk," Jo added.

"Well, at least we figured out who killed Dupont and Richardson. And I have to say it's been great working with you guys. I knew you were a good guy, Sam. I'm glad I was proved right." Bev shook hands with all of them.

"Congratulating yourselves, I see," Holden Joyce said as he strolled around the row of post office boxes.

"We caught the killer, so congratulations are in order," Bev said.

"I heard. But what about this big drug ring? Was it just two guys?" Holden taunted them.

Sam leveled a look at him. "I think you know it was more than two guys."

"So where's all the evidence?" Holden asked.

"Unfortunately, our biggest lead is dead, and the head honcho is smarter than we thought," Bev said.

Holden's eyes narrowed at Sam. "Maybe. Or maybe the police helped obscure some of the evidence. My gut still tells me there's more going on in this police station than meets the eye." He glanced around at all of them, his eyes stopping when they came to Jo. She wouldn't give him the satisfaction of looking away, but she sensed some sort of meaning behind his look. Was it a threat? He moved on to Wyatt, and she let out a breath. "But I'll give you this: you did catch the killer."

"And Tyler Richardson's killer," Bev added.

"Yeah, about the Richardson case. There're still a few discrepancies. Like the fake Fallen Officers Fund." Holden quirked a brow at Sam.

"Oh no. You can't go there," Bev said. "I investigated that, and my forensic accountants determined that Chief Mason gave that money to Tyler's mother out of the kindness of his heart. We followed the money trail. He took it from his retirement fund. Nothing nefarious there. She'd have been too proud to accept it otherwise."

Holden made a face. "That may be so, but there's also the matter of the forged logbook. Our handwriting expert analyzed it. We knew it wasn't Tyler's from the start, but now we know whose it was."

"Who?" Bev asked.

"Officer Harris." Holden turned to Jo again. "You know you can get suspended for that."

"No," Sam cut in. "She did that on my orders, so I'll be the one suspended."

Jo shot up from her desk. "I did that on my own because I didn't want Tyler to have a black mark against his name."

"Surely you can understand that," Bev said. "Or

have you never cared about any of your fellow officers' reputations?"

Holden shrugged. "Sure, but where do you draw the line? It's kind of like harassing people who aren't suspects—like Forest Duncan."

Sam stared at him. "We weren't harassing. We've got to follow every lead. It turns out Duncan didn't have a thing to do with Dupont's murder."

Jo and Sam had talked to Forest Duncan the day after the shooting. They pretended Tyler had told them about how he was working with him to set him at ease. After assuring him that anything he told them wouldn't leave their confidence and Thorne would never find out Forest had admitted that he'd been conducting surveillance on Thorne for Tyler. Unfortunately, he didn't have any evidence against Thorne, only against Scott Elliott.

But Sam and Jo had learned that Tyler hadn't betrayed their trust after all. He'd done what he had to do for his sister. Funny thing was, he wasn't the one tipping off Thorne either. Of course, they couldn't tell Holden or Bev or even Wyatt any of this.

"Don't be such a tight-ass, Holden. Let it go," Bev said.

Holden stared at her, his jaw tight. His eyes drifted to Jo again. "Maybe I will let this one go. I have bigger fish. Don't get too comfortable; you haven't seen the last of me." He gave them one last pointed glare and left.

"Ominous," Wyatt said.

"Overly dramatic," Sam added.

"Can't say I'd be sorry to see the last of him. I hope it's an idle threat." Bev stuffed her wide-brimmed hat on her head. "And on that note, I'll be on my way. It's been great working with you folks, but let's hope a case like this one doesn't necessitate working together again anytime soon."

As Bev walked around the post office boxes, Harry entered.

"Harry, good seeing you again," Bev said.

"You too, Sheriff." Harry smiled at Bev then stepped aside for her to pass. As she continued toward the front door, Harry turned toward them, his smile fading. "I came to apologize again. I really messed up."

"Don't be too hard on yourself, Harry," Sam said. "The EMTs said the compression technique you used on Kevin helped save his life."

"Wouldn't have needed saving if I hadn't messed up and gone there in the first place," Harry muttered. "How is Kevin? Will he ...?" Harry let his voice trail off.

"Don't know. He's unresponsive right now, but we're hoping for the best."

Harry bent down to pet Lucy. "I'm glad you're okay, girl."

"Yep. She escaped with only a few scratches on her nose," Jo said. "Her thick fur protected her."

"Did you get the evidence you needed against Thorne?" Harry asked.

"Didn't get that. But we'll keep trying. Kevin would want us to."

Harry nodded solemnly. "I came with an invitation for you, Sam."

Sam's left brow ticked up.

"Marnie Wilson wants to take you to lunch and congratulate you on arresting Dupont's killer. She said she feels safer now knowing that when she becomes mayor, she'll have a good man like you watching her back."

Sam shook his head. "I didn't do it by myself. Heck, I hardly did anything. It's my team that deserves recognition."

"Oh, well, I'm sure Marnie wouldn't mind taking everyone to lunch."

Wyatt stood from his desk. "You guys go ahead. I have to run out to Rita Hoelscher's. Something about an altercation between Bitsy and Bullwinkle. You know how she is." Wyatt rolled his eyes and headed toward the door.

"See if you can bring back some of that fruitcake!" Harry yelled after him. He turned to Jo. "Jo, what about you?"

The last thing she wanted to do was suffer through a lunch with Marnie Wilson. "No, you two go ahead. I'll stay here and man the fort. Reese is in class all day, and Lucy would be lonely with no one here."

"Well, Sam, I guess that leaves you and me." Harry clapped Sam on the back.

Sam frowned at Jo, looking uncertain. Jo waved him on. "Go. Bring me back a burger or something."

"Okay. Ketchup and mayo?" Sam asked.

"Yep."

"Good. I have to make the most of this lunch," Harry said as he walked with Sam toward the front door. "The wife has me on a short leash. She thinks I'm only having lunch with Marnie. She doesn't want me hanging around here and getting into shootouts. Now she's talking about going to Florida early this year, probably to get me away from here. It's boring. Nothing but Rite Aids and grocery stores. Sitting on the beach all day, a man could grow old before his time down there."

Jo watched them leave then turned to Lucy. "I guess it's just you and me, girl."

Lucy wagged her tail happily.

Jo glanced toward the town offices. Henley Jamison had been thrilled that they'd nailed Alvin Ray. Maybe too thrilled. He'd asked several times if they'd found evidence of any others in the drug ring and seemed quite pleased they hadn't. Could he be working with Thorne, just as Dupont had? If he was, Jo had a feeling that Jamison would know exactly what he was getting into, unlike Dupont, who had gotten in over his head and been killed for it. Jamison would be in the thick of things. Or maybe he was just a pompous ass.

Either way, it might not be so bad having Marnie Wilson in the mayor's office.

Still, there was something about Wilson that set Jo's nerves on edge. And it wasn't the gleam in her eye when she looked at Sam or the way that look made Jo's heart tug uncomfortably. Jo and Sam were just friends; she had no stake there. Why would she care if Marnie was interested in Sam?

Of course, Jo and Sam would still go after Thorne, no matter what. Thorne still had Mick's knife, and even though Alvin was dead, Jo doubted that would slow the drug trade in Coos County long. Sam had already said that if Thorne thought that threatening him with that knife would keep Sam from trying to nail him, he had another think coming. Sam and Mick hadn't done anything wrong twenty years ago, but Thorne had people in high places, and Jo wondered how he could twist the facts to make it look as though they had.

Jo's thoughts turned to Tyler's box, hidden at her house. The contents had answered a lot of their questions. But she couldn't stop thinking about the photo of the beech trees. She'd compared them to the ones from her sister's case, and they were a match. The police didn't think the trees were any indication of where the serial killer had buried his victims, but Jo had other thoughts. And the breaks on the branches of these trees looked fairly fresh, not nearly thirty years old.

Even so, she had no idea where those trees were. Maybe Forest Duncan would be able to shed some light on that, but she'd have to make a special trip to his place to ask him without Sam knowing.

No, that wasn't right. If she was going to investigate her sister's case again, she'd have to come clean with Sam. She'd have to tell him everything, because he'd told her everything about the knife and what had happened with his cousin. She owed it to him. If she didn't, it would drive a wedge between them, and their friendship would never recover. But that was only *if* she pursued the case.

She still wasn't sure. Maybe dredging up those memories of her sister and her relentless, obsessive pursuit of that case wasn't for the best. Sometimes you had to let things go.

Lucy trotted to the back door and sniffed vigorously at the crack in the bottom. She turned and looked at Jo, her lip curled.

"What is it? Is something out there?" Jo asked. She'd only seen Lucy curl her lip when there was a cat around.

Jo opened the door.

Meow.

A large, fluffy black cat, just like the one she'd seen at Alvin Ray's house, peered inside, its luminescent green eyes full of hope. It looked ragged and hungry and reminded Jo of the way Lucy used to look before they'd taken her in.

Lucy growled and looked up at Jo as if to say, "Get rid of it."

"Oh, come on, Lucy, can't you see he's hungry?" Now that Jo looked at the cat, she realized it probably was Alvin Ray's. They'd never seen the cat after that night, even though they'd been back to the house several times.

She'd been worried and had even left a dish of food out for it, but the food had never been eaten. If this was Alvin's cat, it was now homeless. Shouldn't she take it in and feed it and at least get it to the animal shelter? Living outdoors in northern New Hampshire was a hard life for a domestic cat, and any number of wild predators would make a meal of this guy.

Lucy pushed against the door with her nose, trying to shut it.

"Just one little snack?" Jo petted Lucy on the top of her head. "What would have happened if we didn't let you in?"

Lucy sighed and trotted to the opposite end of the squad room, where she plopped down, placed her head on her paws, and glared at them.

Jo felt guilty about the cat. It had been living a nice life until they'd shot up its living room and killed its owner. It was her responsibility to make sure the cat got to the animal shelter.

"Come on in." The cat tentatively stuck a few whiskers over the threshold of the door, and Jo glanced back at Lucy. She didn't look happy, but at least she was grudgingly accepting Jo's efforts to welcome the cat. "I think we have room for another furry friend in here ... at least for a little while."

****

JOIN my readers list to get notification about the next Sam Mason mystery:

https://ladobbsreaders.gr8.com

Books in the Sam Mason Series:

Telling Lies (Book 1)
Keeping Secrets (Book 2)
Exposing Truths (Book 3)
Betraying Trust (Book 4)
Killing Dreams (Book 5)

Did you know that I write mysteries under other names? Join the LDobbs reader group on Facebook on find out! It's a fun group where I give out inside scoops on my books and we talk about reading!

https://www.facebook.com/groups/ldobbsreaders

ALSO BY L. A. DOBBS

Sam Mason Mysteries

***

Telling Lies (Book 1)

Keeping Secrets (Book 2)

Exposing Truths (Book 3)

Betraying Trust (Book 4)

Killing Dreams (Book 5)

Rockford Security Systems (Romantic Suspense)

*Formerly published with same titles under my pen name Lee Anne Jones

Deadly Betrayal (Book 1)

Fatal Games (Book 2)

Treacherous Seduction (Book 3)

Calculating Desires (Book 4)

Wicked Deception (Book 5)

Criminal Intentions (Book 6)

ABOUT THE AUTHOR

L. A. Dobbs also writes light mysteries as USA Today Bestselling author Leighann Dobbs. Lee has had a passion for reading since she was old enough to hold a book, but she didn't put pen to paper until much later in life. After a twenty-year career as a software engineer, she realized you can't make a living reading books, so she tried her hand at writing them and discovered she had a passion for that, too! She lives in New Hampshire with her husband, Bruce, their trusty Chihuahua mix, Mojo, and beautiful rescue cat, Kitty.

Her book "Dead Wrong" won the "Best Mystery Romance" award at the 2014 Indie Romance Convention.

Her book "Ghostly Paws" was the 2015 Chanticleer Mystery & Mayhem First Place category winner in the Animal Mystery category.

Join her VIP Readers group on Facebook:
https://www.facebook.com/groups/ldobbsreaders

Find out about her L. A. Dobbs Mysteries at:
http://www.ladobbs.com